"Go Back To Atlanta,"

Lee ordered curtly. "You and your mile-long limousine don't belong in Graceville."

Caroline hid her hurt and replied sarcastically, "What a nice welcome-home speech, Lee. Did the Chamber of Commerce appoint you as a one-man reception committee?"

"*Rejection* committee. Outsiders aren't welcome here."

Caroline felt her temper fraying. Talk about the pot calling the kettle black! To her recollection, they were *both* outsiders—Lee because of his illegitimate birth, and her because everyone considered her family "poor white trash."

"What's wrong, Mrs. Noble? Cat got your tongue? Or are you tongue-tied because you know I won't be fooled by a pack of lies?"

"When did I ever lie to you, Lee?"

"When did you tell me the truth?"

Caroline lowered her voice until it was barely more than a whisper. "When I told you I wouldn't be back until I was somebody you could be proud of."

Dear Reader,

April is here and spring is in the air! But if you aren't one of those lucky people who gets to spend April in Paris, you can still take that trip to romance—with Silhouette Desire!

You can fly off to San Francisco—one of *my* favorite cities!—and meet Frank Chambers, April's *Man of the Month,* in *Dream Mender* by Sherryl Woods. Or you can get into a car and trek across America with Brooke Ferguson and Pete Cooper in *Isn't It Romantic?* by Kathleen Korbel. (No, I'm not going to tell you what Pete and Brooke are doing. You have to read the book!) And if you're feeling particularly adventurous, you can battle fish, mud and flood with Dom Seeger and Alicia Bernard in Karen Leabo's delightful *Unearthly Delights.*

Of course, we all know that you don't *have* to travel to find love. Sometimes happiness is in your own backyard. In Jackie Merritt's *Boss Lady,* very desperate and very pregnant TJ Reese meets hometown hunk Marc Torelli. Tricia Everett finds that the man of her dreams is . . . her husband, in Noelle Berry McCue's *Moonlight Promise.* And Caroline Nobel returns to the man who's always lit her fire in *Hometown Man* by Jo Ann Algermissen.

So, it might not be April in Paris for you—*this* year. But don't worry, it's still love—at home or away— with Silhouette Desire.

Until next month,

Lucia Macro
Senior Editor

JO ANN ALGERMISSEN

HOMETOWN MAN

SILHOUETTE *Desire*®

Published by Silhouette Books New York

America's Publisher of Contemporary Romance

SILHOUETTE BOOKS
300 East 42nd St., New York, N.Y. 10017

HOMETOWN MAN

ISBN: 0-373-05706-7

First Silhouette Books printing April 1992

Printed in the U.S.A.

JO ANN ALGERMISSEN

lives near the Atlantic Ocean, where she spends hours daydreaming to her heart's content. She remembers that, as a youngster, she always had "daydreams in class" written on every report card. But she also follows the writer's creed: write what you know about. After twenty-five years of marriage, she has experienced love—how it is, how it can be and how it ought to be. Mrs. Algermissen has also written under a romanticized version of her maiden name, Anna Hudson.

One

"Whooeee! Would you look at that!" Hector Jackson pushed aside the dingy red-and-white-checked curtains covering the smudged windowpanes at Gilda's Café. "That's gotta be the longest car I ever seen!"

Amused by the awestruck note in his uncle's voice, Jimbo Jackson glanced in the direction that Hector was pointing his fork. The hushed whispers that had been buzzing since the moment Hector and Jimbo had walked into the café together increased until they sounded louder than horseflies buzzing around a sweet Georgia watermelon.

"Reckon Bobby-John traded in his eighteen-wheeler for something fancier?" Jimbo speculated loudly, pretending not to know who was in the limo.

His grin widened as he heard the scrape of chairs against the linoleum floor. The gossip changed from

"What are those two doing together?" to "Who's in that limousine?" Unashamed of their curiosity or their lack of sophistication, everyone jostled for position near the windows. Jimbo faked a spasm of coughs to cover his chuckles.

His sister was going to love it when he told her what a commotion she'd caused.

"Naw, it couldn't be Bobby-John's," Hector replied as he used his paper napkin to wipe months of accumulated smoke and grease from the window-pane. "Nobody around Graceville could afford nothin' like that. Maybe old man Carson could durin' the heydays of the mill, but nobody's been able to afford nothin' since he croaked and Justin took over runnin' it. Must be some city slicker who's here to buy the mill at the auction."

"Over Lee Carson's dead body," Jimbo overheard Gilda mutter.

The rubberneckers hustled to pay their checks and get out the front door when the limousine slowly turned the corner of the town's square, disappearing from sight. The cowbell attached to the front door began to clang with regularity as Gilda's Café emptied of customers.

Jimbo forked the last bite of fried egg and grits into his mouth. "I can't feature why anybody'd want the mill."

"Birthright," Hector muttered, giving his nephew a shrewd glance. The wily smile on his face reverted to his usual surly expression. Hands flat on the table, Hector flexed his scrawny arms and heaved his sparse body upward. "Lee Carson may've been born on the wrong side of the blanket, but I reckon he's been hankerin' after that mill since he was knee-high to a grasshopper. It'll be a cold day in hell before Lee lets a stranger buy it." He leaned across the table and whispered in a hateful voice, "The same day you git your mama's farm."

Jimbo pointed toward the window. "I'd say that day is closer than you think, Hector. In fact, my guess is that it's about as far away as that limo—just around the corner."

"What the hell you mean by that, boy?" Hector demanded.

With a slight shrug, Jimbo said, "Hector, I've got a feeling the lady in that limo is going to provide more excitement around this town than the last Fourth of July parade when Mayor Caldfield's toupee blew off and landed on Tater's trombone. She's going to shake this town right down to its Confederate roots."

"How the hell you know that, boy?" A crafty look entered Hector's eyes. "You insinuatin' it's Caroline in that limo?" He shoved back the curtains again for a better look. All he saw was the backs of Gilda's customers. Turning, he pointed his tobacco-stained finger in Jimbo's face and blustered, "Don't make no difference if it is her. Caroline married rich, but mark my word, boy, she ain't gettin' the farm. Don't go countin' your chickens before they hatch!"

Jimbo tilted his chair until it rested on its two back legs and steepled his long fingers on his chest as he appeared to ponder Hector's threat. He'd waited a long time to see his uncle get his just deserts. That was the only reason he'd been able to stomach sharing a table with the man. His faith in Caroline gave him the confidence to reply softly, "One chicken...two chickens...three chickens..."

* * *

Tom Smith pressed a button on the dashboard of the Lincoln that lowered the glass between the driver's seat and the two women seated in the plush rear seats of the limo. "Mrs. Noble, I'm unable to locate a parking space that will fit the car. Shall I parallel park?"

"That will be fine, Tom," Caroline replied. Only a hint of soft Southern drawl could be detected in her voice. "You'll have to put nickels in several of the parking meters."

"Yes, ma'am."

Caroline Jackson Noble inhaled a deep, fortifying breath as her chauffeur stopped the vehicle and began backing it across the width of several parking spaces. This was supposed to be her moment of triumphant return, and yet her throat was constricting as she tried to swallow the knot of fear lodged there. Where was the rush of exhilaration she'd expected to feel? Why did her stomach churn as though a million live shrimp were flopping around inside of it? In her conquering-heroine-returns-home fantasy this wasn't how she had felt!

She felt more self-conscious than she had the first day of school. Her eyes squeezed shut as she remembered the kindergarten teacher looking down her nose at the rubber thongs on her feet. She'd been sent home for wearing "inappropriate school attire."

She forced the unpleasant memory to the back of her mind and opened her eyes. Nobody in Graceville could criticize her clothing today. She clenched her fist on the supple navy-blue leather gloves she held.

Badly in need of a friendly smile, Caroline turned toward her personal secretary, Regina Parker, who was eyeing the turn-of-the-century courthouse building as though it were a living dinosaur. "What do you think?"

"I think this town needs a face-lift more than I do," Regina replied dryly. She stroked the slight jowls beneath her chin, then patted her steel gray curls. Bending forward, she glanced out the window next to Caroline and added, "If one more person steps out on that porch to gawk at us, it's going to collapse."

Caroline's facial muscles felt taut as she tried to smile. Gilda's Café had been called everything from a greasy spoon to the Ptomaine Palace by the locals, but for some unknown reason she felt honor bound to defend the shabby diner. "Gilda makes the best biscuits and red-eye gravy you'll ever taste."

"Red-eye gravy?" Regina repeated. Her dark eyes expressed her amusement as she asked, "Does Gilda serve grits, too?"

"With every meal, like them or not. You're in for some real home cooking, Southern style. I haven't tasted a decent mouthful of dandelion greens since I last ate at Gilda's."

"Gravy, grits and greens?" Regina laughed as she squeezed Caroline's hand. Thickening her own natural Southern drawl until it was thicker than peach syrup, she said, "Honey child, I swore off greens, grits and gravy twenty years ago when I moved from Palmyra, Tennessee to Atlanta, Georgia. Your deardeparted husband may have persuaded you to settle up past debts by returning to Graceville to buy the mill and your mother's farm, but I have one request. Can we head back toward civilization *before lunch?*"

"The auction shouldn't last long. I doubt there will be any other bidders." Pausing, Caroline dropped the veil of her hat over her face as she thought of the only other person in town who might be interested in purchasing the mill: Lee Carson.

A vivid image of a tall, skinny, gangly-limbed kid formed in her mind. A smile tugged at the corners of her mouth as she remembered the growth spurts that had perpetually kept his jeans two inches too short. He must stand well over six feet tall by now, she mused.

An intense wave of homesickness flooded through her when she remembered her only true friend. Mutual poverty, neglect and shame had been the glue that cemented their relationship. Lee had helped her cope with each devastating crisis that confronted her. Twice, Lee had offered marriage as an escape route to her problems at home. But while she'd loved Lee, she hadn't been *in love* with him. A loveless teenage marriage would only have compounded both their problems.

But thinking of Lee made her remember the reasons she'd had to escape Graceville and her own home. As she did whenever depression threatened to overwhelm her, she mentally hit the switch that tuned out all the memories, both good and bad. It was a technique she'd devised to keep her sanity during the first few months after she'd left her hometown.

Think only of the present and the future, she silently urged herself. Forget Lee Carson. According to what Jimbo said, Lee had made a fortune in land development. He wouldn't have been able to accomplish anything if she'd continued to drag him down by hanging around his neck like an albatross. Stick to your priority list. Today, the mill. Tomorrow, Whispering Oaks. And in the near future, the Jackson farm.

Determination lit her eyes as she began tugging her gloves in place. She dreaded telling Regina of her immediate plans to stay in Graceville. Undoubtedly Regina would gladly eat a double helping of Gilda's fare before she accepted the fact that Caroline planned on establishing her permanent home in Graceville.

"You'll be out of town by noon. I've instructed Tom to take you straight back to Atlanta after the auction."

"Us," Regina corrected, picking up her briefcase and preparing to get out of the limo. "There's no reason for you to stay here. It'll be weeks, probably months before the mill can be renovated. By then, we'll have put together a top-flight management staff to take over running it. You're going back to Atlanta with me."

Caroline's eyes misted, blurring her vision. She shook her head. Her reason for staying in Atlanta was gone, dead and buried. Dear, dear Carl, Caroline thought, wishing he was beside her. She'd grieved for him sorely during the six months he'd been hospitalized, deteriorating before her eyes. It was during that time of long talks and longer silences that he'd convinced her she should return to Graceville.

"I'm not going back to Atlanta. There's nothing there for me."

"Nothing? What about Carl's department store?"

Caroline blinked back her tears and placed her gloved hand on Regina's wrist. "Carl wanted you to take over his administrative duties, Regina."

"Hogwash! He wanted both of us to take charge of the store. You're running away from Atlanta because of the filthy lies Carl's relatives are spreading around town. It's just greed that has them trying to break Carl's will. Damned vultures!''

"Don't get riled, Regina.'' Caroline glanced through the smoked-glass window at the crowd on Gilda's porch. She'd learned to ignore painful words long before she ever left Graceville. "If gossip was lethal, I'd have died long ago. I couldn't care less what Carl's relatives say as long as I know the truth.''

"You aren't the only one who's privy to the truth. I know why Carl was so determined to marry you. He didn't want to give those vultures a chance to squeeze a dime out of his estate.''

"I owed Carl. Without his guidance we both know where I'd be today—a sales clerk in the designers' boutique at Noble's during the day, waiting on tables at night and sewing on weekends.'' A small smile curved her lips as she remembered how scared she'd been the day Carl Noble discovered she'd had the audacity to wear clothes she'd designed and made by hand to work in the designers' boutique at his store. "Carl could have fired me instead of taking me under his protective wing.''

"Fire the woman who was like a breath of fresh air and sunshine in a department that reeked of stale mothballs?''

"You're exaggerating,'' Caroline protested. "Carl contracted with several of Europe's oldest designing houses.''

"Who hadn't had a new idea in decades,'' Regina added dryly. "Sales went up dramatically when Carl bullied you into putting your talents to work for him.''

"He gave me my big chance.''

"And what did you give him? Until you came into the picture I'd heard him say many a time that he wished he'd died in the accident that left him crippled. You were the reason he clung so tenaciously to life.''

The shaky tremor in Regina's voice brought a rush of tears to Caroline's eyes. She had to do something to get her emotions back in control, otherwise when Tom opened her door the entire population of Graceville would see her bawling on Regina's shoulder.

That was the last thing Caroline wanted to happen. In the worst of times the folks in Graceville had never seen her cry. Not when she'd been seven and her father had been killed in an accident at the mill. Not when her father's brother, Hector, had arrived from the mountains of West Virginia to "take care of his brother's family." Not even after her mother had died when she was fourteen and Uncle Hector had forced her to drop out of school to work at Carson Mill. As in a million and one other small towns throughout the South, in Graceville the truant officer ignored the child labor laws. And at eighteen, she'd still been dry-eyed when she boarded the Greyhound bus bound for Atlanta.

She'd sworn never to return until she could buy the whole damned town. And now she could. The time for tears was behind her. She wasn't about to let them see her cry.

"Are you telling me you don't feel capable of running things in Atlanta?" Caroline asked, knowing Regina prided herself on being extremely competent. "What about the lectures you've given me about carrying on the Noble reputation for fine quality and excellent service? While I'm here carrying out Carl's deathbed wish, are you going to let me down? Let *him* down?"

"No." Regina shook her head. "But are you certain this is what Carl wanted? What you want?"

"Positive," Caroline answered unequivocally. The door beside her swung open. She started to exit the limousine, then paused long enough to add, "Carl loved both of us. His putting you in charge in Atlanta was his way of showing his regard for you. He believed in you, just as he believed I would have the courage to return here."

Inhaling one last fortifying breath, Caroline stepped out of the car into the bright spring sunshine. Her blue eyes darkened with anticipation as she searched for Jimbo's face in the crowd that had congregated at the edge of the sidewalk. No one appeared to recognize her, which for the time being suited her.

Over the years the only person she'd kept in touch with in Graceville was her younger brother, Jimbo. Last night she'd phoned Jimbo from Atlanta to remind him of her arrival. Why wasn't he here to greet her? She lifted her eyes, searching the shadowed recesses of Gilda's porch, and spotted Jimbo leaning against the window. Raising her hand, she waved at him.

Several of the townspeople waved back at her. Milly Jones, the postmistress, and Rose Thornton, who ran the general store, responded as enthusiastically as if Caroline were a Hollywood starlet whose chauffeur had taken a wrong turn on the road to Hilton Head and become lost in the backwoods of Georgia.

Jimbo elbowed his way to the front of the porch, then vaulted over the wooden rail to the sidewalk. His agility took Caroline by surprise. Although she'd paid for the operation on Jimbo's leg, she had continued to picture her younger brother as lame.

"How are you doing, sis?" he asked loudly as he bodily picked Caroline up off the ground and whirled her around in a wide circle. "You're the talk of the town, lady. Breakfast at Gilda's never tasted so good."

Laughing at her brother's wild exhilaration, Caroline hung on to her hat with one hand and gave Jimbo a warm hug with the other arm. As she recovered her balance she noticed several people's mouths hung open in stunned surprise.

"You remember Regina and Tom, don't you?" Caroline asked by way of introduction.

"Sure do." Jimbo pumped Tom's hand heartily and gave Regina a smile of recognition. "The auction ought to start in ten or fifteen minutes. Y'all take good care of my sis at the auction, will you?"

"You aren't coming with us?" Caroline asked, disappointed.

"Can't. It's Friday. Payday. Robert E. Lee would have to arrive in a stretch limo for the boss at the lumber mill to let the payroll clerk play hooky on payday."

"Head accountant," Caroline corrected, nudging Jimbo in the ribs for understating the importance of his job.

Jimbo grinned. "The *only* accountant. I gotta run, sis. Catch you at Carson Mill, later?"

"I'll be there." Caroline smiled at the thought of the two Jackson kids sipping champagne at Carson Mill. They'd both swept floors and strung looms there. In his wildest fantasy, she knew Jimbo had never dared to hope that one day she'd own it.

"Shall I wait for you here, Mrs. Noble?" Tom inquired formally.

Regina poked good-natured fun at Tom's faked regal demeanor by saying, "I think Tom is afraid the natives are going to pounce on the Lincoln and leave a trail of fingerprints on his wax job."

Although she gave the appearance of being properly aloof, Caroline watched Tom's gaze dance roguishly across the faces on the opposite side of the street. "One never knows where one will find unsavory characters, Miss Regina."

Caroline smiled. The friendly bickering that took place between Regina and Tom the moment they were within hearing range of each other never failed to amuse her. Tom was twice Regina's diminutive size and a hundred pounds heavier, but the dirty look Regina shot in Tom's direction made it clear she wasn't about to let him get the last word or the last look.

"Tom had better stay out of the courthouse. Someone might mistake him for one of the men on the Ten Most Wanted posters," Regina quipped.

Caroline missed Tom's retort. Her attention was drawn away by the sound of a black Cherokee roaring down Main Street. Like the Lincoln's, its windows were darkly tinted, which obscured her vision. The truck veered into the parking space in front of the limo, barely missing the front bumper.

"Hey!" Tom shouted, momentarily distracted from Regina's snappy retort. "Watch where you're going!"

A man who dwarfed Tom, with shoulders as broad as an ax handle and hips as narrow as the width of the blade, got out of the Cherokee. Dressed in gray slacks, a white long-sleeved shirt with gold cuff links and a red silk tie, this man couldn't be mistaken for a local farmer. Caroline recognized the cut of a New York-tailored suit without having to examine the label.

The moment he slung his suit jacket over one muscular shoulder and glanced in Caroline's direction, she felt her heart accelerate with unexpected delight.

Lee? Lee Carson!

Caroline was grateful the veil of her hat covered her face. Her jaw seemed to have come unhinged by the changes she saw in Lee. As a kid, Lee's hands and feet had appeared oversize for the rest of his lanky body. Now he stood well over six feet tall, and his proportions were in perfect balance. His face had lost any remnants of teenage roundness. It was all hard planes—hollowed cheeks, square jaw and straight nose.

Almost straight, she revised, remembering how his nose had been broken in a fistfight. Nobody, not even the school bully, made lewd remarks to Caroline Jackson while Lee Carson was around.

She felt a sharp twinge of regret. For friendship's sake, she should have kept in contact with Lee. She hadn't.

Lee stared at the elegant woman dressed from head to toe in navy blue as though he'd seen a ghost. He didn't need to lift the veil covering her face to know it concealed eyes the color of wild blueberries, a pert nose and lips that could melt a man's heart when they smiled at him. He didn't need to take one step closer to know he could tuck her neatly under his arm, even if she was wearing high heels. Nor did he need to hear the soft drawl of her Southern accent for hot blood to rush to his lower extremities.

For an instant Lee dared to hope that Caroline had returned seeking him. That hope lasted for a time shorter than it took him to blink his eyes. Lee had been born on a Sunday, but not last Sunday. Her arrival on the day Carson Mill was to be auctioned off wasn't coincidence. She was here to bid on the textile mill.

And he'd be damned if he'd let her buy it!

Abruptly, Lee ripped his gaze away from the face of the woman who'd haunted his thoughts and dreams for a decade. He'd been a fool over her for too many years to take a chance on letting one of her smiles melt his insides. He wasn't going to let her get under his skin again.

As she narrowed the space between them he fueled the fires of his bitterness by silently repeating her married name. Mrs. Carl Noble. Caroline Jackson Noble. She'd married Carl Noble for the two things Lee had been unable to give her: money and social status.

Aware the whole town was watching her, Caroline reached out both her hands toward Lee. For an instant the sunlight had reflected a warmth in his gray eyes, but then they had changed, hardened, until they shone like polished steel. In the space of a heartbeat the expression on Lee's face had gone from recognition to... anger? No, worse than anger. Hatred?

Her hands moved over her heart as though to protect it. Lee Carson hated her? Why? He'd been upset and angry the day she left Graceville, but that was ten years ago. Of all the people in this town, Lee Carson should have understood why she had to leave!

"Go back to Atlanta," Lee ordered curtly. The angry bitterness he felt made his voice hard, unyielding, loud. "You, your fancy friends and your mile-long limo don't belong in Graceville."

Stung by Lee's hatefulness, Caroline hid her hurt by replying sarcastically, "What a nice welcome-home speech, Lee. Did the chamber of commerce appoint you as a one-man reception committee?"

"*Rejection* committee," Lee corrected. "*Ejection* committee, if that's what it takes to get you out of here. Outsiders aren't welcome to bid on Carson Mill."

Caroline felt her temper fray. Talk about the pot calling the kettle black! To her recollection, they'd both been outsiders—Lee, because of his illegitimate birth, and she, because everyone considered the Jackson family to be "poor white trash."

But whether or not he considered her an outsider wasn't the issue. Her arriving in Graceville to bid on the mill was the issue sticking in Lee Carson's craw.

"I suppose the hometown boy who swore to tear down the mill with his bare hands, brick by brick, is a better buyer than someone who plans to renovate it?" she countered as she edged closer, scowling up at him.

She would have pecked her forefinger against his chest the way she had during squabbles they'd had when they were children, but she didn't trust her finger to perform the task. She had a strong hunch the pleasure of touching the muscular wall of his chest would cause her finger to dillydally.

Her hunch perplexed her. Dillydally? With Lee Carson? Her scowl deepened as she began to see Lee through the eyes of a grown woman. She'd have to be half-blind and cross-eyed not to be impressed by the man standing inches away from her.

"Damned straight," Lee agreed. "This community would much rather watch me tear down the mill than have you rub their noses in dirt."

Acutely aware of her proximity, Lee curled his index finger tighter into the collar of the jacket slung over his shoulder and shoved his other hand deep into his pants pocket to keep his hands from brushing back the loosened tendrils of mahogany-brown hair that had worked free of the pins and curled naturally beside her temples. Her eyes were like blue flames heating his blood, scorching his soul. Every muscle in his body responded to her womanly allure by tensing, screaming for him to pull her into his arms.

Lee staunchly reminded himself that he was an old pro when it came to keeping his hands to himself whenever Caroline Jackson was within touching distance. While other teenage boys grabbed and groped at the girls, he'd been a model of restraint. He hadn't touched her then; he wouldn't touch her now.

"Is that why you think I'm going to bid on the mill? That my owning it is some twisted form of... of... revenge?" Caroline sputtered angrily.

"Can you deny that having the people who once ridiculed you down on bended knees begging for their old jobs won't tickle your fancy?"

"Yes, I can and do deny it."

"Then tell me why you did come back?"

Caroline certainly wasn't going to blurt out the truth, not with everyone stretching their ears to hear what was being said. Lee would laugh her out of town if she told him she'd returned to earn the respect of the people who'd warped her self-image. She needed to prove her worth to herself. She wanted respect. And she was willing to work damned hard to get it!

"What's wrong, Mrs. Noble? Cat got your tongue? Or are you tongue-tied because you know I won't be fooled by a pack of lies?" Lee goaded. He wanted her angry with him. Spitting mad. As long as her temper was out of control she'd be too busy hating him to discover how badly she'd hurt him the day she left him. Ten years had come and gone, but he could still taste the dust in his mouth from the day he'd chased on foot after the bus she'd just boarded. Call it male pride, vanity or just plain old stupidity, but he didn't want her to find out how much he'd loved her.

Maybe, if she thoroughly detested him, her anger would give him the strength he needed to stay away from her.

"I've never lied to you, Lee Carson!"

Lee raised one eyebrow skeptically.

"When?" she badgered. "When did I lie to you?"

The day we nicked our fingers, mingled our blood, and you swore we'd be friends through thick and thin, he silently shouted. The day you promised to write at least once a week, for the rest of your life! He hadn't received so much as a postcard...or a wedding invitation! Damn her sweet-smelling hide, he'd found out she'd married Carl Noble purely by accident. And knowing it had nearly destroyed him!

"When did you tell me the truth?" he retaliated.

Caroline lowered her voice to barely above a whisper. "When I told you I wouldn't be back until I was somebody you would be proud of?"

The way her voice lilted upward, making her revelation a question instead of a statement, struck a familiar deep chord within Lee. For a moment he almost responded to the vulnerability he heard in her voice. The hand in his pocket balled into a fist as though he could physically hold on to the hard kernel of antagonism he felt toward Mrs. Caroline Noble.

"Go flaunt your money elsewhere, Mrs. Noble. I'm not impressed by it."

She inhaled with a sharp hiss before turning away from him. It should have made him feel better to know he had the power to hurt her. God knew she'd done a tap dance on his heart wearing hobnailed boots! But knowing he'd hurt her didn't ease his own pain. He could feel his cheeks redden with shame.

Slightly dazed by Lee's vehement expression of his low regard of her, Caroline had to concentrate on putting one foot in front of the other as she walked back to where Tom and Regina waited for her. Her knees threatened to buckle under her at any moment. She wondered if Lee had voiced the opinion of everyone watching her.

She glanced across the street. Rose had her hand cupped beside her mouth, whispering to Milly. Gilda whispered to the man standing next to her. The others stared at Caroline, their faces lit with anticipation. Her stomach knotted as she inwardly cringed, but her determination to prove her worth stopped her from climbing into the limo and giving the order to return to Atlanta.

Slowly, she started up the steps that led to the courthouse. Each foot seemed to weigh a ton, as weighty as the problems confronting Caroline.

So, what were her options?

There were none, other than outbidding Lee Carson.

"Caroline?" Regina touched her sleeve. "Who was *that?*"

"Lee Carson."

"The guy whose mortgage is being foreclosed?" Regina shrugged. "No wonder he looked upset."

"No. That's Lee's half brother, Justin Carson, who owns the mill. I imagine Lee is here to bid on it." Her stomach clenched into a tight knot when she added, "Lee used to be my closest friend."

"Uh-oh." Regina groaned. "He must have figured out what you're doing here. No wonder he wasn't overjoyed to see you."

Caroline nodded. Some homecoming, she thought. She'd expected a chilly reception from the townspeople; they'd always looked down their noses at the Jackson family. But the hard, cold glint in Lee's eyes had chilled her bones to the marrow.

Her steps faltered. For comfort and guidance, she soundlessly mouthed Carl's last words to her. "Go back to your roots. Sweet tomorrows can't blossom when rooted in sour yesterdays. Be all that you can be, Caroline... all that you ought to be."

Sweet tomorrows? Carl's illness must have affected his pragmatic mind with romantic foolishness. Did she have even the slimmest chance of gaining self-respect? Admiration? Approval? Or would she always look in the mirror and only see "that wild no-good Jackson kid"?

Opening her eyes, she turned to take a good hard look at her hometown to confirm her last thoughts.

Storefronts still lined the square, but half of the plate-glass windows were boarded up, the interiors vacant. Like hundreds of other small towns across America, Graceville was slowly dying from economic starvation. Her troubled eyes moved to the people who'd watched her arrival and now followed her up the courthouse steps as though she were the Pied Piper, who'd play a tune that would change their lives.

Could she make a difference?

Sparks of determination flowed through her, restoring her resolve to reach out and grab those sweet tomorrows Carl had promised. She wasn't the same Caroline Jackson who'd left Graceville—a little nobody bound for nowhere, with all her possessions stuffed in a plastic grocery sack. She was Caroline Jackson Noble. She had a healthy checkbook in her purse and the know-how to make the mill profitable. All she needed was a chance to prove it.

Pivoting on one foot, she marched up the last few steps, mentally prepared to fight Lee Carson or anyone else who stood between her and complete self-respect.

They'd reached the carved oak door that led into the courthouse when Regina placed her hand on Caroline's sleeve. "Don't do it, Caroline. Come back to Atlanta with me. Can't you see that you don't belong here? You've outgrown this town."

For a moment, Caroline wished she *could* choose the easy road that led back to Atlanta, to Carl's posh penthouse apartment that overlooked Peachtree Avenue, to Noble's department store in the heart of downtown Atlanta, where she could walk through the revolving door, stretch out her hand and almost feel the vibrant pulse of the booming city.

Certain she'd be unable to explain to Regina the compelling inner force that made staying in Graceville imperative, she resorted to the kind of irreverent comment Regina would have made if their roles were reversed.

Flashing her secretary a sassy smile, Caroline exaggerated Regina's Tennessee drawl and said, "Cain't leave, honey chil'. Tain't much, and it ain't gonna be easy fixin' it up real purty-like, but it's my hometown. Sugar lump, y'all come visit when you can, y'hear?''

Instead of smiling back, as Caroline had expected, Regina looked momentarily sad.

"You okay?" Caroline asked.

Exhaling heavily, Regina nodded. "If I didn't know better, I'd swear I just felt a stab of homesickness."

"Oh yeah?"

"Yeah." Regina swung the double doors to the courthouse open wide. "Let's get in there and get this over with before I succumb to it. The fresh air around here must be affecting my brain cells. I won't breathe easy until my lungs get a jarring dose of the city's carbon monoxide."

Satisfied that Regina vaguely understood why she was carrying through with her plans, Caroline stepped jauntily through the open door. Once inside she lifted her veil, then removed her gloves.

Brownish water rings on the ceiling and cracked plaster gave mute testimony to the lack of wealth in the entire county. Caroline and Regina moved across the scarred marble floor and down the corridor. Oil paintings of the town's mayors hung in ornate gilded frames.

"Impressive portraits," Regina commented, pausing beneath the last painting in the row. She dusted the nameplate with one finger and read, "Chaucer Carson."

"Yup. The father of both Justin and Lee. Notice the gray Carson eyes."

"What about them?"

Caroline grinned. "They'll be rolling backward in shock after the auction."

"Maybe not. From the financial reports I've read, Chaucer Carson qualified as a bona fide member of the jet set. He couldn't have cared less what happened to the mill. It was mortgaged to the hilt before Justin inherited it."

"Take my word for it. The day the new owner of the mill's picture is hung beside that one will be the same day Chaucer spins facedown in his grave."

Regina nudged Carolina as she glanced toward the doors. "Looks like the townsfolk can't contain their curiosity. We'd better get moving before the courtroom is packed."

Seconds later, Caroline entered the walnut-paneled courtroom and felt Lee's bold eyes on her. Their eyes met and held. Without the flimsy barrier of the veil between them, the full impact of his cold glare sent shivers dancing up her spine.

She hastily ransacked her memories of Lee, seeking some hint, some clue that should have warned her of the raw masculine power he'd exude as an adult male. His tough-guy reputation had always made the other schoolgirls' hearts flutter, but not hers—not then. He'd been special to her, but she'd never felt the bone-jarring physical attraction she now experienced.

Lee Carson had been the only safe haven she had in her tumultuous young life. He had bandaged her scraped knees, listened to her childhood and teenage secrets and comforted her when her world seemed to be going totally crazy. Her lips curved into a wide smile at the recollection.

The smile did it. Lee could actually feel his heart expand as it began to thud loudly in his chest, and unwillingly he smiled. Firmly, he compressed his lips into a thin line.

He'd silently vowed to love her forever the day he'd carved their initials inside a heart on the oak tree near the tidal river. She'd made him break that vow of eternal love. He'd stopped loving her the day she'd married a man three times her age—a man who had one foot in the grave and the other on the footrest of a wheelchair.

Nursing his anger, Lee glowered at Caroline. She could keep her smiles. Or better yet, she could beam them at some other man who had more money than brains. She'd rejected him when he was as poor as a church mouse. She sure as hell wasn't going to worm her way back into his affections.

No, sirree, he thought, folding his arms across his chest and averting his eyes. She'd have to find some other sucker to waltz down the church aisle. He'd break both his own legs before he took one step in her direction!

Two

The judge's gavel pounded three times, signifying acceptance of Caroline's last bid. Although the courtroom had filled to capacity and each bid from Lee and Caroline was met with a flurry of cautious whispers, for several seconds after the final strike of the gavel the room was quiet as a tomb.

Lee tensed. He expected Caroline at any moment to bounce to her feet, give a triumphant whoop and dance a victory jig. When he heard nothing, he glanced over his shoulder. Why was she just sitting there like a bump on a log? She'd outbidden him, fair and square. His lips tightened. He hated her serene poise more than he'd have disliked hearing her gloat. It made him want to vault over the benches and shake her until her sophisticated veneer splintered, until the real Caroline Jackson emerged. He could swallow his pride and accept Caroline Jackson as the new owner of Carson Mill, but he'd never concede to Caroline Noble. Never!

Justin Carson jumped to his feet, clapping his hands, encouraging others to follow his lead.

Caroline hoped the other townsfolk would applaud her acquisition, too. She noticed that a couple of the observers had their hands wide apart, positioned to clap, but they remained motionless, staring from Justin to Lee to herself.

Seconds passed. Caroline's high hopes for instant acceptance plummeted as she watched those people who'd been about to applaud drop their hands to their laps.

Were the townspeople giving her purchase of the mill a thumbs-down reception? Was it respect for Lee that held them in check? Or an unwillingness to follow Justin Carson's example?

Disappointed, but not wanting anyone to realize how much being welcomed back into the fold would have meant to her, Caroline had to remind herself sternly that she wasn't here to win a popularity contest.

She had accomplished her first goal. She owned the mill. Only patience and hard work would earn the respect she desperately wanted.

Her eyes strayed to Lee. As in her own case, the odds had been against Lee being held in high regard. His illegitimacy and his mother's abandonment of him had been millstones around his neck. Chaucer Carson had supported him financially, but never acknowledged him as a son. And yet, Caroline could tell the sentiments of the people who had ridiculed the town's only illegitimate child had completely changed.

The townspeople had held back their applause because they now supported Lee.

From the proud tilt of Lee's head and the square set of his shoulders, Caroline felt certain that he viewed her snatching the mill that should have been his birthright as merely a temporary setback. A lesser man would have bowed his head in defeat. The mark of a survivor, Caroline thought, admiring his profile. It was no wonder to her that Lee had stuck it out in Graceville and made a fortune.

Would she have survived if she'd stayed?

Unwilling to dwell on impossible what-ifs, she rose lithely to her feet. She couldn't change the past, but she could accept it and go on from there. Money couldn't buy respect, not in Atlanta or in Graceville. Respect had to be earned. She had to prove her worth.

She struggled to keep her voice from quavering as she said to Regina, "I would appreciate it if you'd take care of the final business details. I'll meet you at the car."

Regina held up the cashier's check she'd removed from her briefcase. "The price was higher than you'd expected to pay, but I'm certain the judge will accept this. It's considerably more than the ten percent required by the bank."

"Thanks."

Justin approached her, but she delayed him by raising one hand. Head held high and eyes straight forward, Caroline strode to the end of the front-row bench and made a sharp ninety-degree turn. She paused until she heard a few gasps of recognition ripple through the crowd. Her maiden name was whispered back and forth over the pewlike benches.

Deciding this was as good a time as any to state her intentions, she said with quiet authority, "Noble Enterprises now owns Carson Mill. Applications for employment will be accepted within the month, after renovations are started. Top wages will be paid."

No one moved. It was as though she'd spoken in a foreign language that none of the natives understood. An old habit compelled Caroline to look toward Lee. When times were tough, he'd always stood beside her.

Back me, Lee, she urged mentally.

But Lee stood silent, poker-faced.

"Congratulations," Justin boomed as he strode to Caroline's side. He picked up her hand. "This town needs a little fresh blood."

Caroline's head jerked upward. The malicious light in Justin's gray eyes—so similar in color to Lee's—was unmistakable. Justin was gloating because Lee had lost the mill.

"Does the name Caroline Jackson sound like fresh blood to you?" Caroline asked coolly.

His eyes widened in surprise. Too flabbergasted to be suave, he dropped her hand as though the stain of being "poor white trash" would rub off, soiling him. "Hector Jackson's kid?"

"His niece," Caroline corrected. "My father was killed in an accident at Carson Mill. Remember?"

"Caroline Jackson," he repeated, covering his surprise by taking both her hands and giving them a light squeeze. His eyes moved appreciatively over her designer suit. "My, my, my...little Caroline Jackson...all grown up. You've changed, but how could I possibly forget the prettiest girl in six counties?"

Easily, Caroline thought, unimpressed by his attempt to charm her. From the corner of her eye she saw Lee approaching them. She disengaged her fingertips from Justin's light hold.

"I knew you'd be a lovely woman one day, but you've exceeded my imagination," Justin said with a winsome smile. "Will you be staying in Graceville?"

"Yes."

Over Justin's shoulder she watched Lee pass by them. She couldn't let him leave the courthouse without speaking to him. "Lee?"

"Mrs. Noble." Lee controlled his impulse to linger. Walking away from Caroline had never been easy, not even when they'd been kids dropped off at the same school bus stop. With a courteous tip of an imaginary hat, he continued what seemed to be one of the longest journeys of his life.

"Rude bastard," Justin muttered under his breath. "I would have torn down the mill with my bare hands before I would have allowed him to sit behind my father's desk."

Caroline's fingertips tingled. She wanted to wipe the smug smile off Justin's face with the back of her hand. Lee's being a bastard was only an accident of birth. Old man Carson's carnal appetites were known throughout the county. A twist of fate could have as easily made Justin the bastard and Lee legitimate.

"Where will you be staying?" Justin asked, returning his full attention to Caroline. He chuckled. "Somehow I can't picture you staying out at your Uncle Hector's farm."

Before Justin could pry into her personal business, she answered, "The Colonial Inn."

"You can't stay *there.*"

The horrified expression on Justin's face amused Caroline. Compared to the farmhouse she'd called home for eighteen years, the Colonial Inn was a five-star motel.

"I can and am," she replied sweetly.

She tucked her purse under her arm and started toward the carved oak doors. Lee had a head start, but she was determined to talk to him before he roared out of town.

"Well, now, we can't have the new owner of Carson Mill staying in a motel." Justin held open the door for her, then cupped her elbow as she started down the steps. "I seem to recall your being fascinated by Whispering Oaks. Why don't you stay with me?"

Caroline's face drained of color, then turned pink with shame. To hide her reaction, she quickly ducked her head. He'd forgotten her until now. Why hadn't he forgotten what she considered to be the biggest embarrassment of her life?

Sneaking a hasty side glance at him, Caroline felt a wave of relief pass through her. Justin had not only forgotten her, he'd also forgotten the "eighteenth-birthday party" he'd given her the night before she left Graceville. Evidently she wasn't the only unsuspecting dewy-eyed innocent who'd been curious about Whispering Oaks.

"No thanks." At the bottom of the steps, she noticed Lee waiting for her beside the limo. The scowl on his face made her remove her elbow from Justin's light grasp. She didn't want to give Lee the mistaken impression that Justin meant anything to her. "I wouldn't want to impose on you. I'll stay at the Colonial Inn until I locate a permanent residence."

Justin grinned. "Does Whispering Oaks strike your fancy?"

Positive that Justin was dangling his family's home like a carrot in front of a starving rabbit, she refused to rise to the bait. Yes, she wanted Whispering Oaks. It was a major part of the dream she'd woven about returning to her hometown and gaining social prominence in Graceville. Anyone who lived in the Carson mansion was automatically elevated to the top echelon of the social ladder.

But Caroline doubted Justin would sell. According to the financial statement she'd had run on him, he had to sell the mill, but with careful money management he could hang on to Whispering Oaks for a few more years.

"I don't recall seeing a For Sale sign in front of Whispering Oaks as I drove into town. Is it for sale?"

"I might be persuaded to sell it . . . to the right person." He gave Lee a cursory glance, and raised his voice slightly. "Why don't you join me for dinner? Say around sevenish? I'll take you on the grand tour of the old place."

Caroline scrutinized his face. The green flecks in his gray eyes reminded her of flashing dollar signs. Distrust made her wonder if Justin had a hidden agenda.

"I'll be busy at the mill for the next few days," she answered cautiously.

"Tomorrow's Saturday. Surely you aren't working Saturday night."

The engaging smile he gave her, which was meant to start her heart fluttering in her chest, failed. To make certain there were no misunderstandings, she said, "I would enjoy dining at the Carson mansion, but it's only fair to tell you that I'm only interested in Whispering Oaks. I'm still in mourning for my husband."

"My condolences, Caroline. But may I say that you're far too attractive to remain single? Widow's weeds only enhance your natural beauty. Tomorrow night? Dinner? Say seven o'clock?"

Nodding her acceptance, she said, "Seven is fine."

"I'll look forward to it." He gave her a slow smile, one full of confidence. He leaned forward to brush a kiss on her cheek, but Caroline's eyes warned him that he'd be making a big mistake. "Until later, Caroline."

Watching Justin walk away, Caroline smiled wryly. Once upon a time, in her adolescent fantasy, Justin Carson had been the handsome prince who lived in a fairy-tale castle. He'd had everything she wanted, everything she didn't have—money, power, respectability.

And he'd treated her like poor white trash.

She twisted the wide gold band on her ring finger and smiled. Was this why Carl had insisted she return to Graceville? Did he want her to see the people who'd drastically molded her attitudes through the eyes of an adult? Justin was nothing—a big fish swimming in a small pond. And Lee? When had he become the man the locals cheered for?

Lee stepped around the rear fender of the limousine. He'd waited for Caroline, needing to be in the open air, away from Justin and the crowd, when he swallowed his pride and congratulated her on picking up a prime piece of real estate.

After overhearing her accept Justin's invitation, he wanted to shake her until her ears rang. Had she forgotten how Justin had always used Whispering Oaks like a chocolate bar waved under a kid's nose? Women who fell for Justin's ploy left Whispering Oaks in the wee hours of the morning, with only the dirty brown taste of disillusionment in their mouths. Caroline should have learned that distasteful lesson on her eighteenth birthday!

When her wistful blue eyes turned toward him, his lungs constricted until he was short of breath. Silently he ridiculed himself. Caroline was not the only one who hadn't learned from past lessons. Those innocent blue eyes of hers could wound him right to his soul with one tiny glance if he let them. His eyes narrowed as though they were the shield over the window to his soul.

"You paid too much for the mill," he said harshly as he approached. "For that amount of cash, you could have bought my dear half brother, wedding ring included."

"Probably," Caroline agreed, "but I'm not interested in liabilities."

Lee raised one dark eyebrow skeptically. His eyes, as gray and rough as Georgia pine bark, moved to her hands. He snagged her wrist between two of his fingers, then slowly peeled the supple Italian leather off her left hand. His thumb followed her lifeline to her wedding band.

Caroline felt naked, exposed, vulnerable. An involuntary tremor of sexual awareness that left her weak-kneed made her fingers curl around his thumb. It was as though some feminine instinct surfaced, coercing her into grabbing hold of and hanging on to Lee.

No man had ever had this effect on her, none. Not even the boy Lee had once been.

"No calluses," Lee observed dryly, trying to cover the grave mistake he'd made by touching her. Her fingers around his thumb had as great an effect on his libido as any other woman touching him intimately. To preserve his sanity, he dropped her hand as though something far worse than hard-earned calluses marred her skin. "I guess gold diggers can afford expensive hand lotion."

His insult hurt, but Caroline refused to let it show. She squashed the pain centered in the region of her heart by looking Lee straight in the eye and saying, "You know even less about me than you know about running a textile mill, Lee Carson."

"I know all that's worth knowing about you, *Mrs. Noble*. You married a man three times your age. A cripple. His money bought Carson Mill."

"How dare you?" Caroline flared. "You know nothing about Carl or why I married him." She ducked her head and started to pull her glove into place.

Lee glared down at the top of Caroline's head, watching her tug at her glove. He couldn't resist one last parting shot. "What's between us isn't finished, Mrs. Noble. I have something you want that can't be bought with a dead man's gold."

Caroline grabbed the door handle of the limousine, opened the door and climbed in. Damn your arrogant hide, Lee Carson, she silently raged. Her eyes fastened on the back of his well-shaped head as he jumped into his Cherokee and backed out of his parking space. You don't have anything I want! I did not come back to Graceville because of you!

With no one able to see her, she let her knees knock together. Her hands trembled as she shed her gloves. Heart beating unevenly, loudly, she yanked off her hat, tossing it on the seat, then fumbled with the pearls roped around her neck. Only when she'd removed her trappings of wealth could she breathe easily.

Her forehead was hot to the touch as her fingertips soothed her furrowed brow. Lying—even to herself—always resulted in her face turning tomato red. Her hands dropped to her lap.

You do want him, a tiny whisper in the back of her head dared to argue.

She rubbed the back of her neck, trying to erase the thought from her mind. Yes, she'd once loved Lee—but as a friend, only as a friend. Looking at Lee had never made her heart skip a beat. Feeling his eyes on her hadn't made her blood warm to the point where she'd wanted to shake her fingers to stop the tingling sensation.

You do want him, her heart whispered again, louder.

Denying it, she whispered aloud, "I want the mill. I want my mother's farm. I want Whispering Oaks. I want everyone who thought of me as that wild, no-account Jackson girl to respect me. I did not come here looking for a passionate affair with Lee Carson."

She felt less troubled when she put the back of her hand against her forehead. It was cool. She must have spoken the truth.

The door beside Caroline opened.

"Signed, sealed—" Regina handed Caroline the court documentation and a set of old-fashioned keys "—and delivered. You are now the proud owner of a defunct textile mill. At least Lee Carson had sense enough not to bid the price any higher. I had a sinking feeling in the pit of my stomach that you wouldn't have blinked an eye if you'd paid double the price."

Neither denying nor confirming Regina's suspicion, Caroline scooted over to the far side of the seat. Unfolding the document, she glanced at the last page, ran her finger over the notary's raised seal and smiled. "Thanks."

"Don't thank me, please. I also have a gut feeling you've put yourself smack-dab in the middle of a family feud that will make the shoot-outs between the Hatfields and the McCoys look like snowball fights in July."

Caroline dropped the legal papers in her purse and closed the clasp with a decisive click. "Justin won't fight. He thinks he's a lover."

"Your lover?" Regina pried.

"No, but not for lack of trying on his part. Justin follows closely in his father's footsteps. Both of them believe innocent virgins in Graceville were raised entirely for their sexual gratification."

"I watched Justin spreading the charm on an inch thick." Regina frowned. "His half brother had just the opposite reaction. I saw Lee tear out of here just now looking as though you'd served him a king-size helping of greens, grits and red-eye gravy!"

Laughing at the sour grimace Regina made, Caroline shook her head. "Stop worrying. Justin is harmless and I'd trust Lee with my life."

"Humph!" Regina scoffed. "That's what the gingerbread boy and the fly thought when the fox and the spider started their trust-me-I'm-harmless routine. We both know what happened to them!"

Uh-oh, Caroline groaned silently. A double dose of the morals in fairy tales was a sure sign Regina's mothering instinct was on the verge of rising to the surface.

To distract her, Caroline glanced through the side window and asked, "Where's Tom? He's usually waiting for us."

"Don't change the subject, Caroline Jackson Noble. Your name isn't Alice and this sure as blazes isn't Wonderland. What's it going to take to get you back where you belong, in *Atlanta?* A White Rabbit?" Regina opened her door and stepped on the curb. Sighting Tom coming out of the diner, she returned to her seat and said, "Here he comes."

A mental image of a white hare sporting a huge clock had Caroline smiling as she glanced at her watch. Plenty of time. By noon she'd have Tom and Regina on the road to Atlanta, and she'd still have time to change clothes and go out to the mill before making an appearance at Whispering Oaks. Much as she loved Regina's company, she was eager to use the set of brass keys that would open the mill's doors.

Expecting Tom to have opened the driver's door while she'd been woolgathering, she gave a second glance toward Gilda's when she saw he had not. Tom stood on the double white line down the middle of Main Street, glaring at the car. Something was drastically wrong.

Caroline grabbed for the door handle. "Tom?"

"I've been keyed!"

Uncertain what he meant, but from the tone of his voice aware it must have been terrible, Caroline emerged from the limo. Tom crossed to the back fender. Gingerly he touched a deep scratch that hopscotched from the taillight to the rear door of the car.

"Some son of a bitch gouged my car with a key!"

Regina looked concerned. "Do you think Lee was that angry?" she asked.

Caroline's eyes stared in the direction Lee's truck had gone. He had approached her from that side of the car, but his hands had been empty of keys. Instinctively she rejected the circumstantial evidence as she replied, "Don't blame Lee without positive proof. He was always blamed for everything bad that happened in Graceville. I hated it then and I don't like it any better now. Anyone could have accidentally damaged the car. Half the people in town passed it on their way to and from the courthouse."

From the skeptical expressions on Regina's and Tom's faces, she knew she'd wasted her breath defending Lee. To put the situation in its proper perspective, she smiled sweetly at Tom and asked, "Will the engine still run?"

"Of course it will."

"Then you'd better drive me over to the motel. I promised Regina she'd be halfway to Atlanta by noon. I think I just heard her stomach growl."

"That wasn't my stomach you heard," Regina contradicted. "It was the growl a tigress makes when her kitten is threatened. I don't like to admit that Tom was right, but obviously there is a criminal element here in Graceville. I want you to reconsider your decision to stay here by yourself."

Caroline moved back into the car while Tom got behind the wheel. She paused for at least two seconds, then gave Regina a jaunty I'll-never-say-uncle smile. "Okay. I've reconsidered. You're going back to Atlanta and I'm staying here. That's what I want, and that's how it's going to be."

The limousine swerved as Tom jerked the wheel to avoid sinking into an axle-deep rut in the road. Caroline jolted against Regina.

"For heaven's sake, Tom. Do you have to take aim and hit those potholes dead center?" Regina complained loudly.

"Sorry. The ruts in the road around here remind me of the days I drove a tank in World War Two!"

"They remind me of your boss!" Regina braced herself in the seat for the next bump. "She's beginning to sound as though she's fallen back into an old rut. I just hope she won't get hurt when I'm not around to guide her through an emotional mine field."

"I can take care of myself," Caroline replied firmly.

The dubious glance Regina shot her didn't shake Caroline's self-confidence. Justin had tried to have an explosive effect on her emotions, but his charm had fizzled like a wet sparkler.

Her fingers curled into her palm, where Lee's thumb had stroked her lifeline. The impact Lee had on her entire nervous system had caught her by surprise. But she wasn't frightened by the tiny bomblike explosions of sexual awareness that had taken place in the region near her heart. Those peculiar sensations Lee caused intrigued her.

Regina might consider Lee one of the "old ruts" she'd fallen into, but Caroline knew better.

Lee drove his Cherokee through the rear gate at Carson Mill. The wrought-iron gates leading into the front of the building were locked, but wind and salty air had taken their toll on the fence and gate at the back of the property. He parked under a stand of cottonwoods and switched off the ignition.

During the ten-minute drive from town he'd refused to think about Caroline. He'd focused his thoughts on what being low bidder on the mill meant to him. He'd planned on buying the mill for less than what Justin owed the bank, which would have forced his half brother either to get a job to support his lifestyle or sell Whispering Oaks and leave Graceville.

Justin's day of reckoning had been temporarily postponed.

And, if the conversation between Justin and Caroline he'd overheard meant what he thought it meant, Justin planned on cementing his financial future either by selling Whispering Oaks...or by marrying Caroline.

Lee folded his arms across the top of the steering wheel and rested his chin on the back of his hand.

"Caroline." His voice cracked until the last syllable was only a murmur. The day he'd discovered she had married Carl Noble he'd sealed his heartache behind a wall of silence. Caroline's return had broken through that fragile barrier. "Caroline...Caroline... Caroline."

His square chin rocked from side to side as he tried to deny what she made him feel each time he looked at her. Dammit, he should hate her. She'd deserted him. She'd married for money. And she'd brought her checkbook with her when she'd returned home.

His teeth clenched. Then why did he feel like a ringtailed polecat? Why did he want to roll back the hands of the clock to the moment he'd first seen her outside the courthouse and try again? Given a second chance, he might have done everything differently.

He had a sudden mental image of him grabbing her into his arms, whirling her around...and of Caroline giving his face a resounding slap in front of God and everybody standing on Gilda's porch. He cringed inwardly.

Yeah, right, Carson. Given a second chance, you would have made a complete ass of yourself!

Stiff-necked pride wasn't all bad. It had sustained him through the auction. Unfortunately, his pride had bitten the dust when he'd heard Justin oozing charm and Caroline lapping it up.

Exasperated with himself, Lee strummed his fingers on the steering wheel. That was when his pride should have rescued him. It should have given him the impetus he needed to climb in his truck and haul his butt beyond the city limits. But no, he'd stood beside Caroline's limousine like a lackey hoping for a pat on the head.

His pride must have been six feet under, dead and buried, when he heard Caroline accept Justin's invitation. He'd literally seen red. He'd wanted to make Caroline feel the hurt raging inside him when he'd sarcastically lashed out at her.

But Caroline had fought back. Lee's mouth twisted downward. She'd defended her deceased husband. The thought of Caroline loving Carl Noble had knocked the props right out from under him.

He'd had the final word, but telling Caroline he had something she wanted left the taste of ashes on his tongue. He wanted her to come to him, but not to buy the quitclaim deed he held on her mother's farm. He wanted...

He wanted...

"Caroline Jackson," he whispered.

He slumped heavily against the back of the seat. For him, wanting Caroline Jackson was a state of mind, an obsession he'd have to end, because the Caroline Jackson he'd loved no longer existed. He had to deal with the fact that Mrs. Caroline Noble, a sophisticated stranger who only slightly resembled his homespun Caroline, was the woman who'd bought the mill.

"Accept it." His voice cracked as memories of his Caroline collided in his mind with the impact of cymbals crashing together. "God help me, I can't."

His eyes closed. He envisioned Caroline, not in a designer suit, but wearing the cotton gingham dress she'd made for herself to wear on the first day of high school. . . .

Three

————

Lee's heart pumped at double time as he raced along the sandy back road to the path leading through the marsh grass. She wasn't at school! She wasn't at home—no one was there, not even Jimbo! She had to be down by the tidal creek. That was where she always went when her troubles seemed larger than the lone giant oak tree whose gnarled roots clung to the bank.

Be there, he silently chanted, scared something dreadful had happened to Caroline. His eyes were riveted to the high branches of the oak tree. Be there!

At sixteen, physically grown to a man's size, he had long powerful legs that quickly covered the mile or so of winding path. His mind raced faster than his feet. He should have used the pay phone at school to call the hospital at Savannah. Neither his foster parents nor the Jacksons had a telephone. If she wasn't at their special place, he'd have to run five miles back to town to get to a phone! She could be dying while he wasted precious minutes searching for her in the wrong places!

He burst through the dense marsh grass. His heart leaped to his throat when he saw Caroline sitting under the tree with her arms wrapped around her bent legs and her face burrowed against her knees. Her thin shoulders shook. He could hear her gulping for air as she wept brokenheartedly.

Caroline never, ever cried.

More frightened by her tears than by the catastrophe he'd imagined, he felt his throat constrict when he opened his mouth to call her name. "Caroline?"

He watched her back stiffen. Her head was turned away from him, but he knew she was scrubbing the tears off her face.

"Can't a girl have any privacy? Get out of here, Lee Carson. I want to be alone!"

Lee heard her voice quiver. She sniffed, then buried her face in her arms. "Why are you bawling your eyes out?"

"I am not . . . crying. I never cry!"

She was. He could almost taste the salty tears she gulped down her throat. His tongue worked as he tried to swallow. He didn't know what to do. Should he leave? That was what she wanted.

He couldn't move. His legs felt as though they were made of gelatin. He wouldn't. No way was he going to leave her alone.

"Talk to me, Caroline," he coaxed. He inched forward until he was next to her. He bent his knees; his back raked against the oak's rough bark as he collapsed by her side. He lifted his arm to put it protectively across her shoulders, but decided against it. He never touched her these days. Touching Caroline would make those peculiar feelings settle in his stomach. "There isn't anything you can't tell me. Nothing can be that bad."

She raised her head slowly. He could see one tear-drenched eye peeking at him, valiantly blinking to hold back another rush of tears. Unaware that she was doing so, she lightly touched his forearm with one shoulder.

"Oh yeah? It can." She propped her elbows on her knees and dug the heels of her hands into her eyes, rubbing them to stop her tears. When she had dammed the tears from flowing, the reason for them spilled through her mouth. "Uncle Hector is making me drop out of school to work at the mill."

"He can't do that!" Lee protested, outraged. He reached protectively across her shoulders, pulling her tightly against his side. "You earn your keep working at the farm!"

"Can and did. You didn't see me at school today, did you?"

"No, but..." Again, Lee was stymied for words. The mill? Carson Textile Mill? Dammit, his father had no right to hire Caroline! She belonged in school! He cradled her fiercely to his chest. He had one more reason for hating the man who'd refused to publicly recognize him as his son. "That son of a bitch! I won't let him get away with this. I'll stop him!"

Misunderstanding who he meant, Caroline said, "There's no stopping Uncle Hector once he's got his mind set. Mother can't. She's scared to death he'll make good on his threat to put me and Jimbo in an orphanage 'cause he can't support us."

Lee felt her shudder, felt the dampness of her tears through his threadbare shirt. They tore at his gut. He had to do something. But what?

He couldn't promise Caroline he'd stop the mill from hiring underage employees. He might as well whistle in the wind. Nobody would listen to him. Caroline wasn't the only kid who worked at the mill. When it came to enforcing the child labor laws, the whole town blinked their eyes. Why wouldn't they? Payroll checks from Carson Mill paid half the town's bills. Like Hector, his father could do as he damn well pleased and nobody would stop either of them.

Frustrated, Lee rocked Caroline in his arms. There had to be something he could do to help her. A wild idea crossed his mind as her arms wrapped around his waist and her breasts flattened against his chest. "Let's get married."

"Married?" Her hair teased his nose as she shook her head. "No."

"Why not? If you're old enough to hold down a full-time job, you're old enough to be my wife. Mac'll let me work more hours at the garage. We'll find a cheap place to live. You can go to school. Maybe Gilda would let you work at the café after school. We can do it, Caroline."

He held his breath, waiting for her answer. His gray eyes rose toward the cloudless sky. It seemed as though the universe had momentarily stopped. She moved not a muscle. Only the sound of the sea breeze whispering through the tall grass assured him their world had not ended.

Caroline sighed, then straightened until he could see her red-rimmed eyes. His stomach twisted into tight knots. Before she spoke, he knew her answer.

"No."

"Why not?"

"Because I'd be jumping from the frying pan into the fire and taking you with me. I want more out of life than working as a waitress at Gilda's. I want to amount to something." She shook her head vehemently. "Besides, you want to make something of yourself, too. Getting married wouldn't be fair to you, either."

"Nothing's fair. Not Hector making you drop out of school. Not my father's willingness to hire you." *Not being called a bastard by kids who don't even know what it means.* "Life isn't fair, Caroline."

"It sucks swamp water," she muttered, moving away from Lee. "Getting married only stirs up the guck at the bottom."

"What do you mean?"

"Mom and Dad got married young." She crossed her legs at the ankles, drew her knees to her chest and tugged the hem of her gingham dress until it covered them. "Within a year they had me. They both had to drop out of school."

Lee's face turned fiery red. Did she know about those dreams he'd had about her? He couldn't control what happened while he slept. He had a hard enough time pushing them to the back of his mind while he was awake! He wanted to swear on a stack of Bibles that he wouldn't touch her, but thoughts of having her next to him in bed every night silenced him. That, and the growing tightness in his jeans.

"There's birth control stuff," he said, his voice hoarse. From the way Caroline was twisting a lock of her hair around her finger, Lee gathered he wasn't the only one with the jitters. "You know what I mean?"

"Yeah. I know what you mean. That thing all you guys carry in your wallets." She looked at him, wide-eyed and innocent. "You haven't used yours, though."

Lee nearly choked on his own saliva. How'd she know if he'd used it? He could have made it with a girl, plenty of times, if he'd wanted to. He didn't want just any girl, though. He only dreamed of Caroline. He'd been waiting for her to grow up.

He puffed up his chest by taking a deep breath. "Have you been following me around day and night?"

"Uh-uh."

"Then how do you know if I have or haven't used it?"

She lightly touched his arm before she broke the bad news. "'Cause it's been in your wallet so long it's worn a mark on the leather. Get it out. I'll show you."

"The hell I will!" He scrunched his bottom firmly against the ground to keep her from picking his back pocket. "You keep your hands out of my pockets or..."

Caroline gracefully jackknifed to her feet. She brushed the back of her skirt, then planted her hands on her hips and declared, "We fight too much to get married. I'd be married and divorced before I graduated from high school."

"You wouldn't divorce me." He jumped to his feet. "What's mine is mine, Caroline Jackson. For keeps."

"Nothing is for keeps, Lee." Her hands dropped to her sides and balled into fists. Determination lit her blue eyes. "Hector can make me work in the mill for a while, but not for keeps like he thinks he can. Just because I can't go to school with the other kids doesn't mean I'm stupid for keeps, either. I can learn stuff on my own. And when I'm smart enough, old enough, I'll leave this town. Graceville! Ha! Somebody should've named it *Dis-graceville!* That's what it really is. But I won't let Hector or your father or anybody else put me down. I'm going to be rich, Lee Carson. That's one promise I'm going to keep.''

With her chin raised and eyes sparkling like blue sapphires, she convinced him she'd amount to something, be somebody. What scared him was not being part of her plan.

With his determination as keen as Caroline's, he caught her by the back of her neck and lowered his mouth to hers. He parted his lips and swallowed the startled noise she made in the back of her throat.

You're mine, Caroline Jackson, he silently vowed as his tongue boldly parted her lips, tasting her sweet innocence. Mine. I won't let you leave me....

"Leave me be," Lee recanted, as he imagined kissing Caroline. The memory of that single kiss had nearly driven him crazy after she'd left for Atlanta. She'd left still believing they were only friends, when he'd wanted to mean far more to her. He'd wanted to be her husband, her lover.

The sound of an engine disturbed Lee from his thoughts. What could it be? It didn't sound loud enough to be Caroline's limo. Although he knew it shouldn't be any concern of his, he couldn't help wondering.

He yanked his key ring from the ignition and jogged from his truck to the loading dock, where a back door to the mill sagged on its hinges. Only the sorry remains of a five-hundred-pound bale of cotton partially blocked the entrance. Without a sound, Lee climbed over the bale and entered the room where opening machines had once cleaned, fluffed and blended the cotton. He quickly moved through the room, heading for the front door.

Sunlight spilled through the two-story-high windows lining the front of the building. As he skirted behind the antiquated carding machines and roving frames, he saw a dozen hiding places that would easily conceal him. He glanced through a dusty windowpane and spied a moped parked by the front steps. He heard the padlock and chains on the front door rattle and ducked into the alcove that led up a flight of steps to the offices.

Caroline removed her backpack before attacking the rusty chain that linked the door handles securely closed. She coiled the chain neatly beside one of the overgrown azalea bushes that lined the front of the building. She'd dreamed of walking through this door as the owner for ten long years. Feeling like a kid on Christmas morning who examined the colorful wrapping on a gift to delay opening it, she smiled as she dusted the red flakes of corrosion off her fingers to prolong the rush of exhilaration she felt.

Her thumb pressed down firmly on the latch. The door remained closed. Undaunted, Caroline rammed her shoulder against it, once, twice, until she felt it give. The hinges creaked in protest, but the door slowly opened.

She stepped into the largest room in the building, the one that housed the spinning frames, bobbins of yarn and looms. Her eyes adjusted from the bright sunlight to the dimmer interior. Her hand moved to her mouth. This wasn't how she'd imagined the mill!

Although she'd known Justin closed it three years ago, in her mind she'd expected to see the mill as she'd left it. The roving frames should have been drawing out cotton fibers from a series of rollers, putting them on bobbins for the spinning machine. She glanced up, almost expecting to hear the hum of the overhead cleaners that kept the yarn dust free. Her gaze circled past the hulking mass of equipment where now only spiders wove their silken webs. What she saw wasn't the mill as she remembered it. Now, what she saw reminded her of dinosaur bones assembled in an Atlanta museum.

And about as useful, Caroline thought sadly. She pushed the scarf off her hair. It would take days, maybe weeks of backbreaking labor to cart out the ancient equipment. Her eyes moved from the brick walls to the oak plank floor. They appeared in salvageable condition.

"It's mine," she said, finding she didn't care how run-down it was. Tossing back her head, she laughed in pure delight. She executed a series of tiny dance steps as she moved to pick up her backpack. Unlatching the buckle, she held up a bottle of champagne she'd brought from Atlanta. "Hurry up, Jimbo! I want you here to celebrate with me!"

Lee watched her uninhibited delight from his hiding place. She had changed her chic navy blue suit for faded blue jeans, her veiled hat for a flowered scarf, her high heels for well-worn sneakers. With the exception of lipstick, her face was devoid of makeup, and she could have easily passed for sixteen—a time when he'd felt she belonged with him. The sight of her compelled him to step from the shadows into the sunlight.

"Will I do?" he asked softly.

Startled, Caroline felt the champagne bottle slipping through her damp fingers. "Oops!" The twisted paper foil at the neck of the bottle saved her from the embarrassment of having it crash to the floor. Flustered by the realization that he must have seen her childish dance, she blurted, "You scared the living daylights out of me!"

"Sorry." He kept a straight face, but the roguish brightness of his eyes was beyond his control. "Will trespassers be prosecuted?"

She thrust the champagne bottle toward him. He'd asked the same question the day he caught her wading in the creek bordering their property. She'd only been wearing her bra and panties. Then, her knees had knocked and her lips had trembled with cold when she submerged shoulder-deep in the icy water. Now, she suffered the same afflictions, but the cause was completely different. She wasn't the least bit cold. His gray eyes warmed her.

To cover her confusion, she gave the same saucy reply she had given then. "First offenders are only strung up by their thumbs. Second offenders get buckshot in the behind."

"And third offenders?"

Caroline grinned, remembering the tomboyish girl who'd often threatened Lee by puckering her lips and making kissing sounds. Somehow she didn't think giving Lee a big buss on the lips now would have him wiping his mouth and screaming bloody murder! Thoughts of exactly what he might do had her digging her hands into the backpack to find the crystal champagne glasses.

"Third offenders are responsible for opening the champagne and proposing a witty toast," she mumbled, unable to fathom why Lee Carson had this devastating effect on her nervous system.

Lee scowled. Was he being overly sensitive? Or was she slipping the knife between his ribs by subtly reminding him that he'd once proposed to her? He slit the foil, removed the wire that held the cork in place, then pried the bottle open. The cork skyrocketed toward the high ceiling, but Caroline did not look up.

He wanted an answer to his silent questions, so he said, "You'll have to *propose* the witty toast. You've only caught me . . . trespassing twice."

A witty toast? From a nitwit? Caroline dug deeper into the satchel as though procrastinating for two or three minutes...years...aeons...would give her time to gather her wits.

When she heard champagne bubbling from the bottle, splashing on the floor, she held up the glass as though it were a trophy. Clever toasts were at the bottom of her priority list as Lee steadied her hand with the tips of his fingers and filled her glass to the brim.

He came to her rescue by simply saying, "To success."

"To success," she repeated, adding, "yours and mine."

He allowed her to take a sip before removing the glass from her hand. She watched him rotate the stem between his fingers until the faint residue of lipstick marking the rim touched his lips. The dry champagne in her mouth turned honey sweet. She swallowed as he took a sip.

"Even when your success is my failure?" he asked calmly.

"Meaning the mill?"

He nodded.

"I considered not bidding on it for the sake of our childhood friendship." She gave an elegant shrug of her shoulders, then strolled toward the front windows, away from where Lee stood rooted to the floor. "I decided I'd be doing both of us a disservice by withholding my bids. How much experience have you had in the textile industry?"

The feminine sway of her hips had distracted him. "None."

She appeared oblivious to him as she tilted her face toward the windows. Sunlight bathed her pale complexion, giving it a golden glow. "I started here. This was my high school. While the other kids in town were studying English, algebra and chemistry, I was learning about fibers, weaves, textures, dyes, designs...."

"And you hated it," Lee reminded her.

"Poverty has few advocates. I despised everything that had to do with being destitute. Still do." She pointed toward the offices overlooking the work area. "After I moved to Atlanta, I learned the distribution end of the business. I started at the bottom rung of the ladder there, too. Salesclerk. Assistant buyer. Purchasing agent. Advertising. Marketing. Those were my college courses. Take my word for it, Lee, to survive in this business you'd better have multiple rows of sharp teeth and be able to swim faster than the average shark. Had you bought the mill and not brought in outsiders, in less than a year you'd have felt as though you'd been sucked into a shark-infested whirlpool that was way over your head."

He edged closer to her, drawn by the appealing idea of Caroline buying the mill to save him from financial ruin. He shoved his hands into his back pockets to keep them from cupping her face, and bit his lower lip to keep from raining kisses across her cheeks. He wanted to hold her close and tell her that she never had to worry about being destitute again. He'd take care of her just as he'd promised to take care of her years ago.

The scent of hundred-dollar-an-ounce perfume teasing his nostrils brought him back to reality.

She didn't need him to take care of her. He might be able to forgive her for leaving him, for not having faith in him, but not for flaunting her husband's money in his face!

"Let me make certain I understand your self-sacrificing, noble intentions," he said, not bothering to pretend he'd swallowed her fabrication. "From the lofty heights of the Noble Building's penthouse, you heard that Carson Mill was going on the auction block. You assumed that I'd bid on it because the Carson name is painted on the front of the building. So, for my sake and my sake alone, you rushed back to Graceville to save me from tossing my hard-earned money into a shark's tank."

Caroline recoiled as though she'd been slapped. He'd twisted what she'd said until he'd completely warped her explanation. And he clearly thought she was a tramp who'd slept her way up to the penthouse! Since honesty had failed to upgrade his low opinion of her, she decided to confirm it instead.

He thought she was a tramp? She'd show him tramp!

Sashaying up to Lee, she removed the champagne goblet from between his fingers and downed the contents in one long gulp. Provocatively licking her lips, she tossed the glass over her shoulder. The sound of crystal shattering on the oak planks contrasted sharply with the sultry tone of her voice as she crooned, "Honey, I'd hate to see you waste your money on an old pile of bricks. Wouldn't it be easier to let a woman buy it for you?"

She watched a slow twist of a grin replace the puzzled expression on Lee's face. Her heart pounded in her throat. The silver glint in his eyes warned her that she'd made a mistake, a bad one. She should have stuck to being cool and aloof!

Lee snaked his hand around her wrist. This was the Caroline he remembered. She'd given a sexy laugh, but her eyes unmistakably shouted, "Go straight to hell!" In one fluid movement he folded her arms beneath her breasts and tugged her backside snugly against him.

"Wild child?" he taunted, calling her by the pet name he'd given her when they were young.

"Let go of me!" While she tried to pry his fingers from her arm, she swung her leg forward in an effort to give him the swift kick on the shins he so richly deserved. "I said let go!"

Lee dodged her heel, but she did manage to trample his toes with her other foot. "You're a phony, Caroline. An elegant fraud. Underneath those fancy clothes you're still the same woman who thumbed her nose at everybody."

"I don't know what you're talking about."

She squirmed, but quickly decided rubbing her backside against Lee was a bad idea. Roughhousing with a ten-year-old boy was different than scuffling with a grown man.

"You sure as hell do!" Lee chuckled when she stomped at his toe and missed. "Back in grade school...when the kids tormented you...you'd get into trouble just to prove they were right.... You were a wild hellion." His accusation was punctuated by her kicks and jabs. "Dammit, Caroline, I'll let go when you start...giving me some...straight answers to a few questions."

Caroline had the satisfaction of hearing the wind knocked out of him as her sharp elbow met its mark. How's that for a straight answer! she thought triumphantly. His grip loosened enough for her to break away from him. He'd always been stronger than she, but he'd never been faster.

She made it through the door, slamming it behind her in an effort to delay him. Flying down the steps two at a time, she straddled her moped. With a good head start she'd be long gone before Lee could catch her. She moved the kickstand up with her left foot while she twisted the ignition key, then glanced over her shoulder at the closed door.

The moped wobbled as it thrust forward. Instantly she realized something was drastically wrong! One look at the front wheel brought a string of unladylike thoughts to her mind.

Someone had let the air out of her tires!

Four

―

"Sharpest elbows and fastest feet in Georgia," Lee muttered, gingerly rubbing his ribs where she'd jabbed him. She'd always been a scrapper. She'd never taken anything from anybody, even him. His fear that Carl Noble's wealth had turned her into a sophisticated snob started to fade.

The muffled roar of the moped's engine starting nixed any notion he had of catching her. Only the sound of her shouting his name steered him toward the front doorway.

He suppressed a chuckle when he saw Caroline's plight. Fate or a rough brand of poetic justice must have flattened her tires. For once in her life, she couldn't get far if she did run away.

"Need a ride?" he drawled.

"I know what you need, Lee Carson," she huffed, swiping her hair back from her face and shaking her fist up at him. Better to be angry at him than stop to think about her reaction to being held in his arms. "A big fat lip. And I'm just the person to give it to you! Remember the last one I gave you? Only this time it won't be an accident…and I don't care how much you grovel, I'm going to tell everyone at Gilda's who gave it to you!"

Unable to resist provoking her, Lee made a tsking noise. "Here I am, an innocent bystander, offering to help a lady in distress—"

"Innocent, my foot!" She bounded up the steps, prepared to make good on her threat. "It's bad enough that you were caught red-handed trespassing on private property—not to mention manhandling the new owner—but letting the air out of my tires when I'm six miles from town is a dirty, low-down stunt!"

"Sure is," Lee agreed. His chuckle was as far from abject chagrin as Graceville was from Seattle. "Vandalism has never been my style. If I wanted you stranded out here I'd have thrown that toy you call transportation in the back of my Cherokee and disappeared."

"You're forgetting one important detail." She thumped her knuckles on his chest. "You and I are the only ones here. I'm fairly certain I didn't let the air out of the tires. That only leaves you."

"And a flimsy set of tires." Lee sidestepped around her to hunker down while he inspected the tire's tread. "In case you haven't noticed, these tires aren't made for back-country roads. You probably ran over something."

His dark brows suddenly drew together. Where he'd expected to find a nail, he found a two-inch slit in the side of the tire. He scooted to the flattened rear tire. It, too, had been sliced. This was no accident.

"Someone else was here." He braced his hands on his knees, slowly rising as he scanned the immediate area for footprints or tire tracks. "Whoever paid you a visit used a pigsticker on your tires."

Caroline quickly examined the cuts. The blade used on the tires could be the same instrument used on the side of the limo, she thought, instantly putting two and two together. She disliked the answer she came up with. While she'd been talking to Justin, Lee had been on that side of the car. And he was the only other person here at the mill. He was also the only person with a motive for wanting to scare her out of town.

She shook her head to erase the odious thought. Of all the people in Graceville other than her brother, she knew Lee the best. He wasn't a sore loser or a sneak. But then on the other hand, he'd never lost anything to her.

Her mind circled, vacillating between Lee's innocence and his guilt.

"What are you staring at?" Lee asked when he noticed her eyes had dropped to the right-hand pocket of his jeans. He slid his fingers into his snug jeans. He withdrew his pocket knife. "This?"

"Yes."

Caroline recognized the knife. To her knowledge it was the one and only gift Lee's father had given him. Much as she wanted to believe he wasn't capable of an underhanded trick, facts were facts. Lee had a motive, a weapon, and he'd been at the scene of both crimes.

"Hey, I know your nose is out of joint because I grabbed you, but you don't really believe I slit your tires, do you?"

"I don't know what I believe," she shouted. "You've gotten me so damned confused I don't know if we're friends or enemies! First you yell at me to get out of town and then you drink my champagne. You tell me, Lee . . . what am I supposed to think? Did you use your knife on my tires?"

Lee bit off his denial. The stubborn tilt of her chin and the skyward direction of her nose told him she did suspect him. He felt bile rise in his throat. In the old days, she'd been the only one who stood by him when everybody else automatically suspected him of any misdemeanor that happened anywhere in the county. She'd changed.

He jammed his knife back into his pocket. "Okay, *Mrs. Noble*. I'll tell you exactly what I think. You're the last person I want as a friend! You don't know the meaning of true friendship. Friends don't run out on each other."

"That's not fair, Lee. I didn't run out on you, and you damned well know it! I had to get away from Hector . . . from this town . . . from the person I knew I'd be if I stayed here!"

"There was nothing wrong with who you were. You'd have outgrown your rebellious stage just as I did."

Caroline shook her head. "What you and everybody else mistook as rebellion was rage. R-A-G-E! I felt like a wounded animal trapped in a dark cage. Every morning I woke up before dawn wanting to gnaw and claw my way out of the pitch-black darkness. Do you know what happens to animals that are penned up for too long? They go crazy! Or they die! I knew that's what would happen to me if I didn't leave.''

Watching her pace back and forth in front of him, he empathized with her, but her reasons for leaving had nothing to do with her behavior once she reached Atlanta.

"You could have written to me. A postcard saying, *I'm alive and well…wish you were here,* wouldn't have been too much for me to expect, would it?''

Caroline halted midstep and turned toward Lee. "Is that why you're so angry? Because I didn't write to you?''

"How do you think that made me feel?'' He stepped forward; she stepped backward. "I made such a nuisance of myself at the post office that Rose posted a No Loitering sign!''

"Jimbo had my address. Why didn't you get it from him?''

"I did. I quit writing after the third envelope came back stamped Forwarding Address Unknown. You must have moved every two weeks!''

"Do you know how tough it is to get a job with no high school diploma, no references and no car? I practically lived in a suitcase until I got the salesclerk job at Noble's.''

"Jimbo never told me—''

"Because Jimbo never knew. He was fourteen when I left. Do you think I was going to tell him that his big sister was living hand-to-mouth?''

"You could have told me. I wasn't fourteen!''

"What would you have done?''

"Brought you back home where you belonged.''

"And put me back into the cage?" Caroline scoffed. "Thanks, but no thanks. Making it on my own wasn't easy, but at least I had my freedom. I didn't have to work at the mill during the day, tend the fields until dark, cook and clean all night and be rewarded for my efforts by turning my wages over to Hector and watching him spend it on booze!"

"I offered to marry you," Lee bellowed. "What more can a man offer?"

The louder he raised his voice, the more quietly Caroline responded. Feelings of guilt lowered her voice. True, she had had valid reasons for breaking contact with anyone in Graceville, but she should have made an exception for Lee.

"We've had this argument, Lee. Stop and think where you'd be today if I had married you," she reasoned. "Can you honestly tell me you'd have taken the risks necessary to get where you are today if I'd been hanging on to your shirttails?" Before he could reply, she answered for him. "You know you wouldn't have. We'd be one more frustrated family trying to scratch out a living in a town that's economically dead on its feet."

"I'd have made it. If you'd stayed, the only difference between what happened today and what would have happened is that I'd have been the only person bidding on the mill at the auction!" And you wouldn't have married another man and used his money to plaster his name over mine on the front of the mill, he silently screamed.

Caroline stopped retreating and pushed her hands against his chest, hard. "We're right back where we started this morning—fighting over ownership of the mill. Well, I own it! You can just haul yourself off *my* property, Lee Carson!''

"Haven't you forgotten something?" He pointed to her flattened tires. ''You need a ride.''

She shoved him again. Her fiery temper matched his as she shouted, ''You *did* do it! Not out of spite, but to put me at your mercy for a ride back into town! Get out of here! I'll crawl back to town on my hands and knees before I'll ride with you.''

"Don't be pigheaded. You need a ride and I'll give it to you.''

Caroline stepped between Lee and her moped. He'd made her so angry her voice cracked as she yelled, ''Open your ears and let's see if I can get this message through that stubborn, thick skull of yours. I can make it on my own! I don't need you or any other man! Got it?''

"Message received. Loud and clear.'' His heart pounded in his ears as he repeated, ''You don't need me.''

"You got it! Hallelujah!''

"And amen!'' Lee said, striding toward the corner of the building.

Caroline kicked the back tire, wishing it was Lee Carson's rear end. In every fight they'd ever had, regardless of who was right and who was wrong, Lee always managed to get the last word. She watched the spokes of the wheel spin to keep her eyes from following Lee's Cherokee as it sped down the rutted road.

This isn't the first verbal skirmish we've had, she told herself. And it isn't the worst.

Slowly, she raised her eyes. They had a long history of fighting one day and apologizing to each other within twenty-four hours. Their fights had always been like the steam valve on a pressure cooker that cleared the air and kept the pot from exploding.

As she watched the red cloud of dust following his truck begin to dissipate, she realized she'd already begun to regret some of the things she'd said during their heated argument.

Instead of being defensive about not keeping in contact with him, she should have apologized. And she shouldn't have ordered him off the property. She didn't need Lee for a ride back to town, but . . .

"Dammit, I do want him to at least *like* me!" Staring down the road, her frown changed to a broad smile when she saw a trail of dust heading back towards her. "I must not be the only one feeling sorry for losing my temper."

Turning toward the road, she raised her hand to her eyes to shade them from the setting sun. As she recognized Jimbo's truck, her smile faded. She was glad he'd remembered to meet her at the mill, but at the same time she was sorry she wouldn't have a chance to make up with Lee.

"Hey, sis!" Jimbo shouted through his open window as he slammed on the brakes. The truck skidded to a halt beside her. Quicker than Caroline could say jackrabbit, he was out of the truck. "Jeez, you really set the town back on their heels. Everybody at the mill was more interested in talking to me about you than getting their paychecks."

"None of them seemed thrilled about my overbidding Lee on the mill." With a wry smile, she looped her hand in the crook of his arm and tugged him up the steps. "I thought the prospect of my employing them would be better than having Lee tear it down."

"I saw Lee barreling along the road. What was he doing out here?" Jimbo's square jaw jutted forward. "Was he hassling you?"

Surprised by her brother's fierce tone, she squeezed his arm to restrain him from chasing after Lee. "No!"

"Are you sure?"

"Well, uh...we did have a minor disagreement," she replied, wanting to appease Jimbo while still sticking close to the truth.

Jimbo clenched his fist, rubbing his knuckles with his other hand. "Do I need to have a little talk with him?"

"For heaven's sake, no! You used to look up to Lee. Is there something going on between the two of you that you haven't told me about?"

"Nothing important." He stared down the road. As far as he could see there was no indication of Lee returning to the mill. Smiling down at his sister, he said, "The rumor going around town is that he had a couple of investors interested in the property. Lee is real savvy when it comes to turning a profit in real estate. Before I started working at the lumber mill, he asked me if I wanted to go into partnership with him."

Caroline heard the mixed admiration and wistfulness in Jimbo's voice.

"Why didn't you take him up on his offer?"

Grinning bashfully, Jimbo tapped his leg. "I didn't want to slow Lee down with my bum leg. He made the offer before you'd started working at the department store...before my operation."

"You'd have been an asset to Lee, with or without full use of your leg, Jimbo." She tapped her forehead with her finger. "It takes what's up here to make sharp business deals."

"Maybe so, maybe not. I just couldn't see myself letting him carry me along for your sake." His eyes met hers as they paused at the top of the steps. "I thought there might be strings attached to his offer. I couldn't let those strings drag you back here and tie you down."

Caroline smiled as she held out her arms as though checking for puppet strings. "No strings, but I am back, ready to roll up my sleeves and get to work."

Jimbo reached around her to open the door slowly. The rusty hinges creaked eerily. He peered over her head into the dingy interior. "Nothing has changed since the last time I was out here—the only spinning being done was by spiders. I guess they were the only weavers Justin could afford." He looped one arm across his sister's shoulders. "I have faith in you, but getting this place out of the red is going to take more than elbow grease. What is this rumor I heard at Gilda's that Justin might sell Whispering Oaks to you?"

Caroline groaned. "The mill isn't the only place that has bugs. The parking meters must be bugged, too."

"Spiders and bugs aren't the same," Jimbo corrected, chuckling. "And neither of them have ears or vocal cords. Actually, though, I think Justin mentioned selling the house to the banker to get Beau off his back, and Beau told Ralph—just in case Ralph wanted to try and list the house. Ralph told Mason and—"

"Never mind." Caroline laughed. "I get the picture. By now the entire town knows I'll be at Whispering Oaks tomorrow evening."

"Yep." He squeezed her shoulders with affection. "I, for one, don't like the idea of you going out there alone. Justin's reputation hasn't changed over the years."

Caroline stepped out from under her brother's protective wing. "I have changed. I'm not the same gullible kid he tried to seduce and he knows it. He won't try any hanky-panky this time."

"You've changed," Jimbo agreed. "He hasn't. Justin still thinks he's God's gift to every virgin in the county. He'll make a pass at you."

"He knows I've been married. He won't be interested in me." The status of her virginity had not changed since she'd left Graceville, but Justin didn't know it...and she certainly wasn't going to discuss the intimate details of her marriage with her younger brother. She glanced at her wristwatch. Turning toward the door, she said, "We'd better be getting back to town. I want to get the tires on the moped fixed before the garage closes."

Following her lead, Jimbo stepped into the sunshine, glanced at the flattened tires and asked, "What happened?"

"Someone slit them."

Jimbo's eyes moved to the road leading to the mill. "Any idea who did it?"

"It could have been anybody." She patted his cheek to remove the scowl lines on his forehead. "I'll report it to Sheriff Welch. It'll give him something to do for a change."

"Fat lot of good that will do. When it comes to solving crimes, the sheriff is as useless as tits on a boar hog." Jimbo lifted the moped into the bed of his truck. "Don't mention this to anyone, sis. I'll snoop around and find out who did it."

Caroline disliked the idea of Jimbo sticking his neck out to protect her. It felt strange to have their roles reversed. She'd always been the one to protect Jimbo. Under the present circumstances, with Jimbo privy to local gossip and her the outsider, she realized he had a better chance of solving these petty crimes than she did.

"I imagine the same person who flattened my tires probably scratched the Lincoln, too." She watched her brother's fists clench and his eyes narrow. "If you find out who did it, you tell me and we'll go straight to the police station. Promise?"

Jimbo shook his head. He moved around the back of the truck to the passenger's door. "Hop in, sis."

"I'm not going anywhere until you give me your word that you won't take the law into your own hands."

"That's how things get done around here and you know it. You've changed, but Graceville hasn't. Get into the truck."

"Jimbo-o." She drew the last vowel sound out to an ominous threat.

Stubborn as his sister, Jimbo said, "I don't make promises I won't keep."

For several seconds Caroline tried to stare him down. When she realized they looked like matching bookends—hands on hips, legs slightly spread, chins tilted—she acquiesced with a small grunt. "Sometimes you can be a pain-in-the-you-know-what, little brother."

Jimbo gave her a cheeky grin as she climbed into his truck. "I was just thinking the same thing about you."

They were halfway back to town when Jimbo said, "Hector was with me at Gilda's this morning. Do you want to drive by the home place?"

"No. I've had enough excitement for one day without confronting Hector." She studied her brother's profile. Jimbo disliked Hector as much as she did. The small muscle ticking along Jimbo's jawline made her wonder what they were doing together at Gilda's. "I'm surprised you two are speaking to each other."

"I wanted to see his reaction to your arrival."

"Which was?"

"Predictable. He doesn't like the idea of you being back in town. He swore you'd never get the farm."

"Do you think Hector might be the one behind the vandalism?"

"Maybe, but I doubt it. I'd have seen his truck."

"He could have used one of the loggers' trails that lead to the back of the mill."

"Maybe." Doubt hung heavily in the momentary silence. Jimbo nudged her arm and shifted the conversation back to the farm. "I drove over to the home place last fall at harvesttime. Hector had planted a few acres, but he never was much of a farmer."

No free labor, Caroline thought, clenching her teeth together. Hector couldn't plow a straight row and wouldn't hoe the weeds. But she'd been able to. He was a strong believer in the back-hills philosophy that the reason a woman had children was so they'd take care of their parents. Since Hector had literally stepped into her father's shoes at the time of his death, he'd felt entitled to the same benefits.

"He has no right to be living on the farm," Jimbo said bitterly. "It belonged to Mother's family."

"She left it to him in her will."

"Yeah, I was only ten when she died, but I knew he'd bullied Mother into writing it. He was always threatening to call child welfare and have us picked up if she didn't do what he wanted. She was too proud to tell anyone, much less ask for help. After she passed away, he held the same stick over your head, didn't he?"

Caroline nodded. "My one fear when I ran away from home was that Hector would follow through on his threat."

"You couldn't take me with you."

"I wanted to. I was so scared of Hector's temper. I used to have nightmares about the time he pushed you off the porch and broke your leg. We should have told Mother what happened."

"We couldn't. We were afraid he'd hurt her and she was afraid he'd hurt us." Jimbo shuddered. "I guess his being afraid I'd follow you is what made him decide to treat me better. Without either one of us at the farm he didn't have anyone to do the work. At least I got to finish high school."

"With honors," Caroline added. "You should have let me pay for you to go to college. I could have afforded it."

"I had to stick around here. Hector threatened to give the farm to charity if I left town." He glanced at the hard set of his sister's mouth, then reached across the seat and gave Caroline a brotherly pat. "Your getting the Jackson farm back is something Mom would have liked, too. I'd say Hector's days of manipulating us are near an end."

"I don't know about that, Jimbo. I'm not sure if I can get it back. I had Regina call the records department because I didn't want anyone to know I was making inquiries. Marybeth told Regina that there aren't any liens on the property."

"Marybeth must be mistaken. The bank wouldn't lend Hector a dime unless he used the land as collateral."

"Monday I'll check the records myself."

Jimbo chuckled. "Haven't you forgotten something?"

"What?"

"Everybody has their eyes on you. Unless you want Hector sitting beside you in the records office you'd better let me take care of that, too."

"Don't you have to work?"

"I asked the boss for a couple of days' vacation." He grinned at Caroline. "It looks as though I'm going to need them. You need all the help you can get out at the mill. What are your plans?"

"I'll be on the phone Monday making arrangements to get everything in shape at the mill. I want a structural engineer to go over the building to check the electrical wiring and the plumbing. I noticed some tuck-pointing needed to be done on the brickwork. There are some interior walls I want moved so I'll have to contact an architect, too. Which reminds me. Tomorrow night I'll ask Justin if he has the original building plans for the mill."

"I wish you'd stay away from Justin until I find out who is trying to scare you out of town."

"You suspect Justin?" she asked skeptically. "I can't visualize him dirtying his hands to cut my tires."

"It's his mill you bought. Justin didn't know what to do with it when he owned it, but I could understand him having the same feelings about it that you and I have about the farm. Neither one of us will farm it, but it's part of our heritage. It's our birthright.''

"What about Lee's birthright? Everybody knows he and Justin are half brothers.''

"Yeah, Lee wanted the mill, too." He strummed his fingers on the wheel thoughtfully and murmured, "It's a shame he wasn't the legitimate heir. The mill would be in full operation. You'd have stayed in Graceville. By now the two of you would probably have a couple of kids scampering on the lawn at Whispering Oaks.''

"Whoa there, little brother! Your imagination is running away with you.''

"Is it? I saw his expression when he first laid eyes on you today. He looked as though you were the angel on the Christmas tree come to life.'' He nudged her elbow and teased, "And I saw how you were looking at him in the courtroom when you thought no one was watching you. The temperature skyrocketed. Didn't you notice Milly Jones and Charity Blankenship break out their paper fans?''

Caroline turned her face toward the window. She could feel her cheeks turning pink. They'd passed the city limits sign before she muttered, "He does have a tendency to make me hot under the collar. I'll have to admit that.''

She pressed her lips together in a manner that signified she wasn't going to explain further. She wasn't proud of her behavior, but she wasn't going to tell Jimbo that Lee's insinuation that she was a gold digger had had the same effect as setting a match to a stick of dynamite. Her temper had exploded. She'd thought she'd outgrown the defensive mechanism of showing somebody she could be worse than they imagined, but she hadn't. Bold as brass, she'd played the role of a female sugar daddy and offered Lee the mill.

And that was when he touched me.

Her backside tingled as she recalled the sensations of being held tightly against him. He had the strength to overpower her, but he'd only exerted enough to restrain her flailing arms and legs.

What would Lee have done if she'd played the role of gold digger and turned around in his arms? Would he have kissed her?

She pictured herself looping her arms around Lee's neck, imagined the surprised look on his face before his arms tightened around her waist and his mouth slowly descended toward her lips.

What would she have done?

Kissed him! Again and again and again.

Caroline's lips turned downward. She couldn't lie to herself. Her emotions had been in total upheaval. She wouldn't have allowed him to kiss her while she was pretending to be a gold digger.

I'd have bitten his lip, she admitted silently. Hard!

"Would you?" Jimbo asked, shaking her arm to gain her attention.

Startled from her introspection, she stared at Jimbo as though he'd read her mind. "Would I what?"

"Would you like me to drop you off at the motel before I have your tires fixed?"

Caroline glanced at her watch. The thought of sitting in her room alone with nothing to do was unappealing. "Do you think it will take long?"

"Maybe, maybe not. I doubt that Mac will have the right size of inner tubes. He'll have to patch the holes."

"Why don't I walk on over to Gilda's and order a couple of hamburgers smothered in onions? My treat."

Jimbo grinned. "Nothing like sticking your head in the lion's mouth, huh, sis?"

"More like tweaking the lion's tail. I gave the folks the glitz treatment this morning. Limo. Designer clothes. Et cetera, et cetera, et cetera." She glanced down at her faded jeans and scuffed-up shoes. "I think it's time to shake them up again. Let them wonder who has moved back to Graceville—Caroline Jackson or Mrs. C. J. Noble."

"I'll say one thing for you. It's never boring when you're around. I'll get there as quickly as I can. I don't want to miss anything."

"You won't." She grinned mischievously. "I'm going to be utterly charming."

"Like I said, I'll hurry."

Five

"**W**ell now, as I live and breathe, it's Caroline Jackson!" Beau Blanton, president of the Graceville National Bank, pushed back his chair, stood and gestured for her to join him at his table. Overweight and balding, he looked every inch the prosperous banker in his custom-made three-piece suit. A large diamond solitaire on his smallest finger matched the one holding his silk tie in place. "Welcome back to Graceville."

Caroline swiftly glanced around the café before deciding where to sit. Each customer had his place: socially elite at the right front, white collars in the center and blue-collar workers at the left front. The misfits belonged in one of the booths along the back, next to the doorway leading to the kitchen.

Her glance halted as she saw Lee sitting alone in the booth they'd often shared. She made a soft, startled sound deep in her throat when the gray intensity of his eyes swept over her. As far as she was concerned they could bash walls down with each other's head in privacy, but in public they'd be civilized to each other. They'd lived by that code of conduct in the past. Caroline saw no reason to change it.

She smiled brightly at Lee.

"Won't you join me?" the banker asked congenially, drawing her attention back to him. He pulled back a chair for her to be seated.

Caroline wasn't fooled by Mr. Blanton's cordiality. He conducted more business at Gilda's than he did in his walnut-paneled office at the bank. She, too, had a hidden agenda. Lunch with Beau Blanton would give her an opportunity to unravel the mystery of why there were no liens recorded on her mother's farm.

She noticed that three chairs at the banker's table were empty. Those seats had always been reserved for Mason Caldfield, the bank's attorney and the mayor. The prospect of shuffling the usual seating arrangements amused Caroline.

"You don't mind if I have a friend join us, do you?" she said. Before Beau Blanton could say yea or nay, she sat down and called to Lee, "Come eat lunch with us." When Lee nodded his acceptance, Caroline directed her attention back to the banker. "Jimbo will be with us in a few minutes."

Beau snapped his fingers to gain Gilda's attention. "Gilda, how about some iced tea for Caroline?"

Caroline gritted her teeth as Gilda instantly started to cross the width of the café, leaving Rose Thornton, the general store owner, in the middle of placing her order.

"Sweetened or plain?" Gilda asked Caroline.

"There's no rush, Gilda," she said. "When you've finished taking Miss Thornton's order, I'll have my tea plain."

Caroline caught sight of the passing frown on Beau Blanton's face. Her reward for being considerate of Gilda and Rose came from an unexpected source... Lee Carson. His gray eyes lit warmly with approval as he took the seat across the table from Beau and next to her. She and Lee had both spent too many years beneath the bottom rung of the social ladder to slight anyone.

"Rose is one of the bank's customers, isn't she?" Caroline said pleasantly. "I wouldn't want her closing her account because of me." It pleased Caroline to watch the banker run his finger between his stiff white collar and his neck as though it were choking him.

Beau cleared his throat, waved at Gilda dismissively and said, "Sorry, Rose. I didn't see that Gilda was taking your order. Like the little lady said, there's no rush." Directing his attention back to Lee, he held out his right hand. "How is the land-developing business, Carson?"

Lee gave Beau's hand a firm shake and replied dryly, "As we all know, I had a deal fall through this morning."

"You don't appear overly upset at the loss," Beau commented.

Lee plucked the laminated menu from between the chrome-plated napkin holder and the ketchup bottle and handed it to Caroline. A master of disguising his feelings, he shrugged his shoulders and replied mildly, "Carson Unlimited will survive without the mill."

She took the menu from Lee's hand. Their eyes met at the same moment she felt his leg press against her knee. Her eyes widened as a little surge of heat spread down her leg to the tips of her toes.

The table is small, but not *that* small, she thought, while her heart picked up its natural tempo. Lee had plenty of room for those long muscular legs of his. Was this his way of silently communicating an apology? Was he as eager to end the hostilities as she?

She raised the menu until the banker could no longer see the lower half of her face and mouthed, "Truce?"

Lee nodded, smiled, then dared to reach under the checkered tablecloth and pat her knee with his hand. When Caroline put her napkin in her lap and covered his hand with her own, he inwardly gave a tremendous sigh of relief.

He'd wanted to hate her for forgetting him, but fighting with Caroline left him hollow inside once his anger had subsided. It always had.

"Guess we're all glad it was a woman who grew up right here in Graceville who bought it," Beau said loudly. "Nothing like a success story to brighten my day, Caroline. Tell me what you've been up to since you left our fair town."

Without glancing around, Caroline sensed from the stillness in the café that everyone was holding their breath, cocking their ears in her direction while they waited for her response. She decided she might as well satisfy their curiosity with the truth.

In case those listening had conveniently forgotten that Hector had forced her to drop out of high school, she answered, "It's tough getting a decent job without a diploma. The first few years I held menial jobs—washing dishes, cleaning houses, baby-sitting. The nights I didn't work, I went to school. You can't imagine how good I felt when I passed the graduate equivalency exam.''

The banker kept a straight face while she spoke, but she heard audible gasps from the others around her. She felt a tremor in Lee's hand before he removed it from her knee. Out of the corner of her eye she caught a glimpse of his lips as they compressed into a tight line.

Lee shuddered at Caroline's candidness. Had she forgotten how showing the smallest amount of weakness would make her vulnerable to the gossip mongers? By the time her story had been repeated dozens of times, the truth would be distorted beyond recognition.

He nudged the side of her foot with his shoe in an effort to stop her monologue.

Caroline shifted her position and crossed her legs to avoid having Lee kick her shins to get her to shut up. She knew exactly what she was doing. Secrets made juicy gossip. Straight facts only made boring news.

''My big break came when I was hired as a salesclerk in the designer boutique at Noble's department store,'' Caroline continued. ''Thanks to the self-improvement policies at Noble's, I earned a bachelor of arts degree in textiles.''

She paused, giving Gilda a friendly smile as the waitress placed a tall glass of iced tea on the table with one hand and refilled the banker's glass with the other. Caroline almost giggled when she saw Beau glare at Gilda for interrupting her story at a crucial point.

''Ready to order, Mrs. Noble?'' Gilda asked. ''The special today is beef pot roast, with the choice of two vegetables, and peach cobbler for dessert. 'Course you might not want to order the cobbler 'cause you'll be having it tomorrow night.''

"I will?"

Flustered, Gilda thumbed through her order tickets. "Well, uh . . . yeah. I mean, I guess you are. Sadie, the cook at Whispering Oaks, phoned here asking if I'd have time to bake some peach cobblers." Her mumbling ceased. A choice piece of gossip deserved to be loudly announced. "Justin wanted something special for dessert 'cause you're going to be eating at Whispering Oaks.''

A rash of whispering broke out at the other tables. Caroline felt the hairs on her neck prickle. Without looking, she knew Lee was casting a smoldering look in her direction.

"In that case," Caroline said, smiling up at Gilda, "I'll have a cheeseburger with the works and fries. Twice."

"Two burgers and two fries?''

"Jimbo will be here soon."

Gilda grinned. "You'd better make that three burgers, with a chocolate malt to wash them down with. Jimbo does have a king-size sweet tooth. I was just saying to him the other day that if he didn't watch out he'd be outgrowing his britches. Speaking of britches—" she eyed Caroline's stonewashed jeans "—it's good to see you looking like you belong here. I was just telling my husband, J.W., that I scarcely recognized you all dressed up in those Sunday-go-to-meeting clothes you were wearing this morning."

Beau interrupted Gilda's spiel by droning, "Gilda . . . the hamburgers." For Caroline's sake he watched his manners and begrudgingly muttered, "Please."

"Just being friendly, Mr. Blanton." Miffed, Gilda shoved her order pad into her apron pocket, turned and shouted, "Three cheeseburgers, two fries and a chocolate malt, J.W."

Beau waited until Gilda moved toward the kitchen, then asked, "Where were we before Gilda got her tongue going ninety-to-nothing?"

At the best part, Caroline replied silently. Aloud, she said, "I became the buyer at Noble's, which led to my starting a line of designer clothing."

"Noble's?" the banker repeated. "Didn't I hear Gilda call you Mrs. Noble?"

Lee leveled his eyes on Beau Blanton, giving him a warning look. To stop Caroline from being quizzed about her husband, Lee considered dumping the remains of the banker's blue plate special into his lap.

"You did." She made a mental note to ask Gilda to call her by her first name. "I married Carl Noble. I'm a widow."

"You're awfully young to be a widow." Beau shook his head as though he'd been a personal friend of her deceased husband. "Was your marriage blessed with little ones?"

"No. No children," she replied. Without batting an eyelash, she explained, "Carl was your age, Beau. We devoted ourselves to making each other happy. It was Carl's suggestion that I consider buying Carson Mill. Of course, he left the final decision up to me."

Lee felt as though he'd been stabbed with a dull knife. Happiness? He'd offered to marry her, to protect her, to provide for her, but he'd never offered Caroline happiness. He looked over at her bleakly.

"We're glad you made the right decision," Beau boomed jovially. "What's good for the mill is good for the town. You're going to make a whole lot of people happy by giving them an honest day's work.''

Caroline lifted her tea glass in silent salute to Beau's sentiments. She'd taken the first step to being accepted in Graceville. That was what she'd always wanted. And then she looked at Lee, and saw the anger smoldering in his eyes. Her heart sank. Lee would never forgive her for buying the mill.

But she had no idea of what to do to appease that anger. Nothing short of seeing his name on the property deed seemed to be acceptable to him. He wanted the one thing she couldn't give him. Until Lee could accept her as the new owner, she'd have to be wary of him.

''You'll need a payroll account here at the local bank so people can cash their checks,'' Beau said, getting down to business. ''You'll find us most cooperative.''

Caroline smiled at Beau's directness. The banker had been born with a silver spoon in his mouth and he wasn't about to let anyone else eat off his plate unless they paid an interest rate higher than they would have to pay doing business elsewhere—which brought her to the reason she'd accepted Beau's offer to be seated with him. She was ready to pay the interest and the principal on Hector's notes.

Testing Beau's cooperativeness, she said, ''Since you brought up business, I do have a little matter that needs to be taken care of immediately.''

She set her glass on the tablecloth while she watched Beau's eyes light up as though she'd punched the dollar button on Gilda's cash register. Lee, on the other hand, looked fit to be tied. She wanted to reassure him that she hadn't totally lost her mind. She'd bury her cash in a tin can behind the mill before she allowed Beau to handle her business accounts. But with all eyes and ears at the diner focused on her, she couldn't very well wink at Lee to let him know she was only dangling the carrot in front of the banker's nose.

"Do you need to transfer funds from Atlanta into a new account?" Beau asked hopefully. He glanced around the café, then leaned toward her. "A loan?"

Caroline noticed the scraping of knives and forks had ceased. Not a single hushed voice could be heard. Everyone listened.

Except Lee. He opened his mouth to tell her that unlike the president of Graceville National Bank, the officers at his bank in Savannah knew the meaning of confidentiality. But then he noticed the gleam in Caroline's eyes. He covered his mouth with one hand to keep from laughing aloud. Beau thought he was being wily as a fox, when in actuality, it was Caroline who was being foxy.

"I'd like to buy any outstanding notes on the Jackson farm that the bank holds." Reaching for her purse to get her checkbook, she heard a couple of chuckles and coughs coming from behind her.

Iced tea spilled from Lee's glass as he purposely sent it flying. Only Caroline's quick reflexes saved her from getting drenched. She pushed her chair back from the table and jumped to her feet.

"Gilda!" Beau shouted. "Get over here!"

"It's my mess. I'll clean it up," Lee said, countermanding Beau's call for help. "Did I get any on you, Caroline?"

Before she could answer, she felt her breasts instantly respond to Lee's touch as he dabbed at the front of her blouse with his napkin. Her nipples tightened as his knuckles brushed against the lacy contours of her bra. Her lungs forgot how to expand and contract, leaving her breathless, speechless.

Answering his own question, Lee said matter-of-factly, "Only a few drops. I'd better get you to the motel before the fabric is stained permanently." He turned toward the lunch counter. "Make those burgers and fries to go, Gilda."

Caroline was thoroughly distracted by the commotion, but Beau wasn't. "Good idea, Carson. There's nothing much I can tell her about the farm other than that Hector paid off the notes."

That jolted Caroline into a quick recovery. She shot Lee a get-your-paws-off-of-me glare, sank back into her chair and bunched the tablecloth until creases of cloth prevented the tea from dribbling on her jeans.

Lee glared down at the top of her head. He'd made himself look like a clumsy oaf for nothing. The only way he'd pry Caroline out of the diner so he could explain about the farm in privacy would be to yank her up by the hair on her head and drag her outside!

And then, he silently fumed, she'd be too damned fired up to listen to me.

Caught between a rock and a hard spot, Lee had little choice other than to sit back down, shut his mouth and keep his ears open. Later, when the whole damned town wasn't listening, he'd have his say.

"Hector paid off the notes and you don't know where he got the money from?" she asked in total disbelief.

Beau nodded. "He paid in hundred-dollar bills, as a matter of fact. He had a wad of them big enough to choke a Clydesdale horse!"

"Hundred-dollar bills?" She glanced at Lee, who had a bland know-nothing expression on his face, then back at the banker.

"I joked with Hector by asking if he'd dug up and sold the family silver your momma's relatives hid from Sherman during the War Between the States." Beau grimaced. "But you know your uncle. He curled his lip, shoved the bank receipts in his overalls pocket and shuffled through the revolving door. I figured I could gently twist a few arms and find out where he got the money. Never did. Whoever gave Hector the money must have made him swear on a stack of Bibles never to tell anybody anything."

Caroline frowned and glanced at Lee. She noticed his gray eyes dancing with mirth as he watched the banker. No wonder the other customers had laughed. Beau's "gentle arm-twisting" and criminal extortion had a lot in common. This had to be the one and only time a secret had been kept in Graceville.

Anxious to compare notes with Jimbo, she glanced at her watch, then through the front window. Evidently Beau hadn't twisted Jimbo's arm, or he'd have told her so while they were driving into town. Turning to the counter, she saw Gilda setting paper sacks on the counter.

"It's been informative talking to you...Beau." She'd be damned if she'd show him deferential treatment by calling him "sir" or "mister." "If you'll excuse me, I'd better go see what's delaying Jimbo."

Lee beat Beau to his feet, and it was Lee's hand that assisted Caroline from her chair.

"I'm going that way," he said in a tone that didn't allow for any argument. "I'll walk you down there."

Beau Blanton extended his hand toward Caroline. "It's been a real pleasure talking to you, Mrs. Noble." When he saw Lee reach into his pocket, he dropped his hand and said, "No, I insist on picking up the tab. Be my guest."

Not willing to be in debt to the banker in even the slightest way, Lee tossed a twenty-dollar bill on the table. "Tell Gilda to keep the change."

While Caroline waited at the counter for Jimbo's malt to be fixed, she realized Carl would have chuckled with pleasure had he been able to hear the discussion that had taken place. Carl had loved seeing the tables turned on people. He'd certainly proved that fact when he'd disinherited his snobbish relatives and left his estate to her. By the same token, she knew he'd have loved hearing about those hundred-dollar bills, too. Carl had loved unsolved mysteries.

"Here you go, Mrs. Noble," Gilda said, handing Caroline two brown paper bags. "Three cheeseburgers, two fries and a chocolate malt."

The fragrance of grilled onions and fries made Caroline's mouth water. No one fixed burgers like J.W. did. "I'd feel like a hometown girl again if you'd call me Caroline."

Gilda grinned, covertly glancing at the banker to see if he'd overheard the request as she gave Caroline her change. "Will do... Caroline. And I'll make certain that peach cobbler gets out to Whispering Oaks."

Less than two minutes later, Lee walked beside Caroline as she headed toward Mac's garage. He waited for her to ask him if he had any knowledge of Hector's good fortune. It irked him that she thought the banker was better informed about Hector and the

Jackson farm than he was. But what really got his goat was Caroline's going out to Whispering Oaks.

His temper was on the rise when he said, "And here I always thought you were a smart kid. Guess I must have been wrong."

"What do you mean by that crack?" Caroline asked warily.

"Nothing much, except that I try to learn from my mistakes. Funny, but I seem to recall the night of your eighteenth birthday as being a major turning point in your life. Have you forgotten it?"

"I haven't." She could feel her face tingling with humiliation. Her first inclination was to grab the bags of food Lee was carrying for her and spring away from him. But she'd been running from home truths most of her life. She had to face the foolish mistakes she'd made without being embarrassed. Now was as good a time as any to show Lee Carson she was streetwise. "You'd invited me to go with you to Savannah to the movies. I chose to go out to Whispering Oaks for a 'surprise party' given by Justin in my honor. The surprise was that I was the only guest, and Justin's birthday present to me was a brief tour of Whispering Oaks. One that started and ended in his bedroom."

"Which you declined, if memory serves me correctly." Lee sensed Caroline would either kick him in the slats or make a mad dash for the garage when he posed his next question, so he took her lightly by the elbow as he leaned down and said softly, "Doesn't going to a cozy dinner for two at Whispering Oaks qualify as making the same mistake twice?"

"I'm going to see the house," she snapped. "Period."

"That's how Justin lured you there the last time."

"There is one major difference, Lee. I'm going there as a prospective buyer. He won't lay a finger on me."

"Right," Lee droned skeptically.

"You're prejudiced. You and Justin have never gotten along. Give me one good reason I should let your dislikes sway me from getting something I've always wanted."

"Because Whispering Oaks is only symbolic of what you really want. You've always craved respectability. But you didn't have to leave Graceville to gain respectability, and you sure as blazes don't have to own Whispering Pines to get it. You can't buy it. Respectability is earned, Caroline."

"I suppose you think you're living proof of that theory!"

"I am." Lee watched Caroline chew on her bottom lip, then shrug her shoulders. "What did you just shrug off?"

"The years it took for you to gain everybody's respect. I don't want to go back to square one." She lifted her chin defiantly. "And I don't *have* to go back to square one. In case you haven't noticed, everyone at Gilda's was sitting on the edge of their chairs, listening to hear what I have to say."

"Curiosity mixed with envy. It won't last. In a week your splashy arrival will be old news. You'll be on the outside, with your nose pressed against the window like a sad little puppy, wondering why nobody associates with you."

Caroline heard Lee's words, but in her heart she held on to the belief that anyone who lived at Whispering Oaks automatically led a charmed life. Old beliefs were hard to shake. In fact, what Lee had said was tantamount to blasphemy. Did he really believe owning Whispering Oaks would not help her attain respectability? Or was this sour grapes she was hearing?

"Tell me the honest-to-God truth, Lee. If Justin offered to sell Whispering Oaks to you, would you refuse to buy it?"

Lee shifted the bags of food to his other arm, taking a moment to consider how to answer. He could flat-out lie and tell her no, or confirm her belief by answering yes. He chose a middle path.

"Our situations are different, Caroline. Your father didn't own Whispering Oaks."

Smiling at Lee's equivocation, Caroline said, "So you would buy the house?"

"I didn't say that."

"Okay. You didn't. So, you wouldn't buy it?"

"I said our reasons are different."

Mimicking him, she drawled, "Right. Owning Whispering Oaks would legitimize your claim as a member of the Carson family, giving you the respectability you were denied as a child. You'd buy it." She snapped her fingers. "In a heart's beat. And so will I."

"You're forgetting about Justin's reputation. His reasons for getting you out there haven't changed. Do yourself a favor and let me set up an appointment for you through a real estate broker."

"Like I said, you're prejudiced against Justin. I imagine his reason for wanting a private deal is simple. By selling it himself, he won't have to pay a broker's commission."

Lee lengthened his strides, feeling as though he was rapidly losing ground. He trusted Justin about as far as he could throw a steel vat full of dye.

Local gossip told him that women found Justin extremely attractive. The man had sown his wild oats all over the county. Begrudgingly, Lee had to give Justin credit for making certain there were no gray-eyed children sprouting up faster than pine trees as proof positive of his half brother's virility!

Lee's mouth turned downward in disgust. He couldn't risk letting Justin get his hands on Caroline. At his wit's end, he did what he felt he should have done ten years ago.

"I forbid you to go to Whispering Oaks."

"You what?"

He held up his hand to forestall the outrage he saw in her eyes. "Let me rephrase that. You are going to decide going out to Whispering Oaks would be unwise."

"Putting thoughts in my head isn't one whit better than giving me orders." Caroline stepped in front of him and jerked the bags of food from under his arm. "I'll go where I damned well please! You can't stop me."

"This time you have my word. I will stop you, Caroline. You can count on it. My word is as good as money in the bank."

Six

The next evening, Caroline carefully steered her moped up the oak-lined lane leading to the Carson mansion. As soon as the trees' shadows enveloped her, the twilight changed to darkness, so she switched on the headlight. The inefficiency of the single beam of light made her wonder if the general consensus that her choice of transportation was crazy had merit.

Eccentric, she silently revised, remembering Carl saying that money was the yardstick that measured the difference between being crazy and eccentric.

The moped had been one of Carl's many gifts to her. Because he was restricted to his wheelchair or to riding in the back seat of the limo, he'd wanted to enjoy vicariously the freedom only a bike allowed. With the wind whipping the silky loose ends of her hair that streamed from beneath her safety helmet against her nape, and the fragrance of wisteria that twined around the giant oaks teasing her nose, she wished she could have shared those glorious sensations with him.

As she spied Lee Carson's truck blocking the lane and her heart did a somersault, she knew the affection she held for her husband was tame in comparison to the wild fluctuation of emotions Lee caused. There was no safe middle ground with Lee, the way there had been with Carl. She either wanted to kill Lee or kiss him.

Slowly braking the bike, she stopped beside the open tailgate where Lee sat with his muscular arms folded across his chest and his legs crossed at the ankles. Determined not to let him rile her into misbehaving, she lifted the visor on her helmet and stated the obvious. "You're blocking the lane."

Lee's slate-gray eyes flicked over her. She was dressed in a chic jumpsuit, the likes of which couldn't be found locally. Although it was demure with its long sleeves, high collar and loose-fitting trousers, the liquid gold fabric gave the illusion that Caroline had been dipped in precious metal.

Sexy as sin with those nips and tucks, he thought, unable to stop himself from taking notice of how the cut of the material drew attention to the shapeliness of her breasts. He found himself wondering what, if anything, she was wearing under the tantalizing garment. Silk with lace plain cotton?

His mouth grew as dry as cotton. He had to pull a tight rein on his imagination by reminding himself that he was here to save Caroline from being seduced, not to be the seducer.

"So I am," he replied quietly. "You aren't going to Whispering Oaks."

"Think again, Lee. I go where I please, when I please and with whom I please."

"In that case, it's going to please you to turn around and go back down the lane with me."

Raising one eyebrow, she scoffed, "I should break an appointment because you think I can't handle a business transaction without Justin seducing me?"

Lee heard the moped's engine roar as she turned her front wheel toward the shallow ditch. Lithely he swung one leg over the moped's front fender, straddled it and snagged the chrome handlebars in his hands.

The rear wheel spun and spit sand.

Caroline spit, "Move."

Lee deftly removed the ignition key. The engine died, as did the headlight. "You're coming with me, like it or not."

"You know, Lee, that has always been one of your problems—ordering me around." Containing her fury, she swung her leg over the side of the moped and nudged the kickstand into place. "How would you respond if I said, 'You're coming with me, like it or not'?"

Lee grinned. "Pick the place."

It suddenly dawned on her that Lee coming with her was a good idea. Should Justin have any amorous intentions, Lee's glares would cool Justin's ardor. "Whispering Oaks. I insist that you be my escort!"

Lee physically backed up from the bike and mentally backed away from her idea of what had to be a joke. "You're kidding."

"No, I mean it, Lee. Come with me." She grinned as a memory struck her. Once, when the Carsons had been on vacation, she'd dared Lee to sneak around the house with her and peek in all the windows. They'd barely circled the house when the security guard found them and escorted them none too gently through the front gates. For weeks they'd talked about their escapade. She put out a hand and touched him on the arm. "You're as curious as I am. Admit it."

In the near-darkness, with only a few evening stars beginning to shine through the sprawling branches of the trees, Lee silently admitted to being...curious. Curious about the electrical sensations pulsating up his arm. Curious about the provocative fullness of Caroline's lips. And still curious about the amount or lack of undergarments beneath the fluid fabric that swished like silk when she moved.

Caroline prompted, "This is your big chance, Lee. The two of us meandering through every nook and cranny of Whispering Oaks is a dream come true. Come with me. I know it's what you've always wanted."

"You don't know a damned thing about what I want," Lee replied, his voice thick with his private desires.

"I do. You wanted the mill and the house. We talked about them millions of times. Come with me...please."

"We shared other dreams." Compelled by her touch, he inched closer. Dreams only you can make come true, he silently added.

The persuasive gentleness of his voice caught Caroline off guard. She'd been so intent on convincing him to go with her, the tingling in her fingers where they touched his arm had gone unnoticed. Her hand slid farther and farther up his arm the closer he came. The difference in their heights diminished as she watched his head bow.

Sane reasons for not wanting him to kiss her resounded in her mind as her body yielded to his taut frame. He wanted the mill. He'd physically prevented her from going to Whispering Oaks because he didn't have faith in her ability to ward off Justin's unwanted attentions. He thought she'd left Graceville to find a rich doddering old fool to marry her.

Dammit, no, she wouldn't kiss him while he believed her to be an unscrupulous gold digger!

She turned her face aside. Undaunted, he pressed a string of kisses along the side of her neck. Her eyes closed as his teeth closed around her earlobe. Dizzy from tilting her head back, she clung tightly to his arm to keep her balance.

"Lee, no." She could barely hear her own protest. Her voice was thick and raspy with suppressed emotions. "No."

"Yes. Forget Whispering Oaks." His lips strayed along her hairline to her widow's peak and on to the opposite side of her face. Her head tilted, giving him access to the vulnerable curve of her neck. His arm looped around her slender waist to support her as he cradled her against him. "Forget the mill. Forget everything other than how you make me feel."

"Can you forget?" she entreated.

With her trembling in his arms, Lee only remembered how right it felt to have Caroline in his arms where she belonged. Could he forget? Forgive her for deserting him, for marrying another man? The dull ache that had surrounded his heart since her departure grew painfully acute when he started to deny his ability to forgive and forget. He'd built his fortune on risk, but he couldn't risk the consequences of saying no to her.

His mouth covered hers. They'd kissed a thousand kisses in his imagination, but his imagination was puny compared to the sweet taste of her as he felt her lips parting beneath him now.

She tastes of peppermint toothpaste, honey and spice—her own special flavor, he thought as he rubbed his tongue across hers. When she responded by nipping him, gently sucking, his whole body felt as hard as the oak trees lining the dark lane.

His hands moved from her waist to cup her breasts through the shimmering gold fabric. His thumb traced along the scalloped edge of her bra, answering one question, then skimmed over her diamond-hard nipples to answer any doubts he had regarding her response to him.

Caroline knew she had to stop him. And she would stop him. In a moment or two. Or three. She wouldn't lock her arms around his neck. No, she definitely would not.

She did.

She wouldn't let his fingers knead her breasts until they felt heavy and hot.

She did.

How long had she been back in Graceville? A little more than twenty-four hours? She wouldn't let him flick open the row of cloth buttons from her neck to her waist.

She did.

Her head was spinning. She didn't know right from wrong, yes from no, doing from not doing.

She wanted him to touch her, wanted it with a passion that shocked her. With each bold thrust of his tongue inside her, her primitive instincts warned her that she wasn't the only one rapidly losing all sense of where they were and what they were doing.

At any moment Justin could drive up the road to see what was causing her delay.

"Lee . . . we have to stop," she whispered shakily when Lee came up for air. She felt his mouth, moist and hot from their kisses, travel down her throat. "Justin . . ."

Lee jerked his head up, pulling her against him to shield her nakedness from his half brother's eyes. The primitive urge to blind anyone who looked on his woman surged through him. "Where?"

"No . . . no, I mean . . ." Dizzy and confused by Lee's reaction, she wedged her hands between them and tried to button her top. "Justin isn't here . . . but he . . ." Her fingers shook so badly she couldn't get the small buttons into the proper holes.

Lee hauled a deep breath into his lungs to quiet his pounding heart. His entire body felt as though his skin had turned inside out and caught fire. He'd lost control, something he seldom did, especially with a woman. The only saving grace he felt was when he looked at Caroline and saw that she was equally shaken by the passion that had flared between them.

"Here," he offered. He pushed one button through its hole, but couldn't complete the simple task when he raised his fingers to the button that, once closed, would cover the cleavage between her breasts. Unable to resist, he placed a fleeting kiss on the soft round-ness, then steeled his nerves to get the slippery fabric closed.

Caroline let him. She had to let him. The kiss he'd bestowed on her breast had sent a new wave of tremors through her hands. She felt like a bottle of champagne that had been thoroughly shaken and uncorked!

To break the uncomfortable silence growing between them, he joked, "Whoever said 'out of sight out of mind' was wrong. The sight of you is permanently imprinted on my mind."

And always has been, she thought she heard him say, but she couldn't be certain.

Trickles of light from a slow-moving car danced along tree trunks and the roar of a high-powered engine prevented Caroline from asking Lee what he'd meant. He'd turned his back on her to confront the intruder.

Had she always been on his mind? Her face turned crimson over how rarely she'd thought of him. Like a willing amnesia victim, she'd tried to forget her traumatic childhood. She'd blocked the good memories along with the bad ones.

Frowning, she hurriedly worked to finish rebuttoning her clothes. She regretted Justin's intrusion, and yet, simultaneously, she felt a sense of relief. Although Lee had said he could forget what had occurred during the span of years she'd been in Atlanta, she wanted him to know the whole truth.

The timing is always wrong, she despaired silently. It's like marketing wool coats in June. Telling Lee the reasons for her marriage had to come before, not after, a bone-melting burst of passion, didn't it? Biting her lip, she watched the lights creep closer to Lee's truck. She'd have to wait. Her shaky fingers pushed the last button through the buttonhole.

"Are you covered up?" Lee asked, glancing over his shoulder at her. His whole body continued to throb with the force of his desire. He chalked up one more reason for disliking Justin.

To make one final check, her hands fluttered across the front of her jumpsuit, then flew to her hair. Her appearance might be restored, but her composure suffered when she noticed his eyes following the path of her hands. "Yes."

Lee silently groaned as he imagined Carl Noble's hands following a similar course. Thoughts of another man eliciting her passionate response had been the cause of many a nightmare. Tormented by a resurgence of those images—only this time with his half brother in the leading male role—he blurted, "I'm going to take you up on your invitation."

"You'll go through Whispering Oaks with me?" she asked in surprise.

A slow smile lifted one side of Lee's mouth at her reaction. She'd had the same excitement in her voice the last time she'd convinced him to go to Whispering Oaks. It pleased him to see occasional glimmers of the old Caroline.

Confident that Justin would never let him put one foot inside the house, he teased, "Yeah. With one stipulation."

"Which is?"

"Don't offer to buy it for me."

Remembering how she'd taunted him at the mill, she retorted with the same spunkiness, "Outbidding you two days in a row? No thanks. I'm ready to compromise. If you want Whispering Oaks, you can have it, with my blessing."

Both of them turned toward the blinding light when they heard the sound of a car door slam. Justin strode toward Lee, his clenched fists making his intentions clear.

Wanting to defuse a potentially explosive situation between the Carson men, Caroline stepped toward Justin and called, "Hi, Justin. Sorry I'm late, but I waited for my real estate specialist to meet me here. You don't mind setting an extra plate for dinner, do you?"

"You invited *him?*" Justin roared. "That bastard!"

"I did." Caroline found it one hundred percent easier to confront Justin than to argue with Lee. Perhaps, she silently conjectured, that's because I'm no longer infatuated with Justin. She did find Lee awesome, though. She placed her hand in the crook of his arm. His forearm flexed with controlled tension, but he didn't charge forward like an enraged bull who'd had a red flag waved in his face. "He's the local expert in real estate."

"I might make you a legitimate offer myself," Lee goaded softly, his voice deliberately icy.

Justin bellied up closer to Lee. "I'll rot in hell before I sell Whispering Oaks to you."

From the slow-spreading smile on Lee's face, Caroline guessed Lee found that idea particularly pleasant. Only his change of stance warned her that he'd also relish the opportunity to flatten his half brother's aristocratic nose.

"From what I've heard, it's Whispering Oaks that's rotting," Lee countered. "You'd better take any offer you can get and consider yourself lucky...again."

"Again?" Justin sneered. "What the hell do you mean by that remark?"

"You know exactly what I mean." Lee disengaged Caroline's hold on his right arm. "All our lives folks have said you were born on the lucky side of the blanket." His smile broadened. "I remade the bed, though, didn't I? The blanket has been flipped to the other side. You're the one who is down on your luck."

Feeling as though she were standing between the Hatfields and the McCoys while they took potshots at each other, Caroline raised her hands for a cease-fire. "Gentlemen, let's get back to business, shall we?"

"I don't do business with him," Justin replied after pausing a couple of seconds.

Hesitation is death, Caroline thought as she recalled the basic rules for negotiating a business deal. Despite Justin's outward bravado, she'd heard the gritty notes of panic underlying what he'd said. She'd been in business situations with high-fashion designers on the brink of financial disaster because their exclusive name meant more to them than a high sales figure. She wanted Whispering Oaks more than she'd wanted those exclusive labels, but Carl had skilfully tutored her on exactly how to respond to Justin's bluff—walk away.

"Whispering Oaks isn't the only house in Graceville." She glanced up at Lee. "I'm sorry to have inconvenienced you by dragging you out here at night. Shall we go?"

Aware of her ploy, Lee suppressed a joyous chuckle and said, "There's a home overlooking the Intracoastal Waterway that might interest you. I can show it to you tonight."

"Your house?" Justin laughed. "She'll hate it. It's nothing like Whispering Oaks."

Lee cast a dangerous glance over his shoulder at Justin. The man has no idea how lucky he is, Lee thought. For two cents—hell, for free—he'd be delighted to punch Justin in the face. Only the feel of Caroline linking her fingers to his hand prevented Lee from losing the tight grip he was maintaining on his temper.

"I'd love to see your home," Caroline said.

"Wait j-j-just a damned minute," Justin sputtered. "Aren't you being a bit rude? What about the dinner invitation you accepted?"

The teenage brashness she'd built her reputation on threatened to resurface as she whirled around to face Justin. He expected polite etiquette after the ill-mannered way he'd spoken to Lee? Hair flouncing, chin jutting forward, eyes shooting fireworks, she was tempted to tell Justin where he could shove his dinner, in no uncertain terms.

But to do so would destroy the sophisticated image she'd created. She quickly blunted her sharp tongue with a sticky-sweet cheerful reply. "You have an extra big helping of Gilda's peach cobbler for me...with my compliments."

Lee chuckled. Her voice might be sweet, but her body language shouted what she privately thought: she wanted to scream, kick Justin's shins and scratch his eyes out—precisely what she had attempted to do the first time she'd heard Justin called Lee a bastard.

"My daddy used to say that you can't change a sow's ear into a silk purse," Justin said with a smirk. Spinning on his heel, he stomped back to his car. "You won't get a second invitation, Miss High and Mighty. You're going to be sorry. Damned sorry!"

Unafraid of Justin's threats and undaunted by his low opinion of her, Caroline had the audacity to wave gaily at him when he jumped in his car and started backing up the lane.

"Is that a sophisticated version of the standard obscene gesture?" Lee teased, feeling euphoric that Caroline had chosen to stand by him.

"How'd you guess?"

"I could hear your back teeth grinding together."

"Ladies don't grind their teeth," she said loftily. To further substantiate her claim she added, "It's in my etiquette book. Page 274, far right-hand column. It comes after under no snoring, no fingernail biting, no stomach growling, no—"

"You memorized an etiquette book?"

Caroline laughed at the stunned expression on his face before she gave his cheek an affectionate pat. "No gaping mouths. Merchandising isn't the only thing I learned in Atlanta."

She thought she saw a flicker of pain cross his face. With the headlights retreating, she couldn't be certain. She decided she must have been mistaken when he turned to her moped and shook his head.

"Does your etiquette book approve of those contraptions?"

"Definitely. Page six."

"Be careful, Pinocchio, I think your nose is starting to grow."

"Wrong page?"

"Wrong book. I think you must have been reading the advertising brochure for the moped." Faking a deep sigh, he crossed to the moped and steered it toward the tailgate of his truck. "Other than flat tires, maintenance on this thing can't be much of a problem. Most of the miles it travels aren't registered on the speedometer because it's always inside the bed of somebody's truck."

"I don't mind. Do you?"

Come to think of it, he didn't. It meant he'd have her company during the drive to his house. If she'd had a car, he'd have been deprived of that pleasure.

"Nope. I don't."

He maneuvered the vehicle until he could close the tailgate. After brushing the dirt off his hands he put his arm across her shoulders and walked her to the passenger's door.

Caroline smiled up at Lee as he opened it for her. Before she stepped on the running board, she gave him a quick peck on the cheek. "Thanks."

"For what?" he asked, shutting the door behind her.

Through the open window, Caroline reached out to touch his face. She traced the bow of his lips with her thumb as she replied, "For all the doors you've held open for me that I rushed through without thanking you. I'm truly sorry I didn't notice you standing there, waiting for me to grow up."

"Apology accepted," Lee said, feeling his heart expand in his chest. He'd never admit it to another living soul, but he felt positively giddy. He had to restrain himself from jumping up and clicking his heels!

Anxious to whisk Caroline away from Justin's clutches and her dream house, Whispering Oaks, he hurried around the truck to the driver's seat.

"My refrigerator is empty," he said, once he'd swerved his truck toward the highway. "Do you want to go to the drive-up window at Gilda's? Her

Southern-fried chicken is still the best in town. I might even be able to wangle a dish of peach cobbler."

Caroline avidly studied his profile as she wondered why Lee had suddenly started to chatter like a magpie. Was he as nervous and excited as she was? Although she sat perfectly still, her insides felt shaky, as though she were nearing the brink of discovering something utterly wonderful.

"Anything you order is fine with me," she murmured.

"Anything?"

"I'm not picky about food. Carl used to say I'd eat beef rare or charred. As long as the chef removed the moo and it didn't stampede off the plate, I wouldn't notice how it was cooked." She expected Lee to laugh. When he didn't crack a smile, she said, "We're going to have to talk about Carl sooner or later, Lee."

"Later," he replied succinctly.

He turned off Main Street into the alley that led to the rear of Gilda's Café. Slowing to a stop, he waited for the car ahead of him to move forward.

"When do we discuss my marriage, Lee? Tomorrow? Next week? Next year?"

"Never is too soon for me."

He'd spent the majority of the night awake, preoccupied by his fear that Caroline continued to be infatuated with Justin. That was why he'd blocked the lane leading to Whispering Oaks. She'd dulled those fears by returning his kisses. She'd utterly destroyed them when she'd sent Justin back to the house to eat an extra helping of peach cobbler. He'd be a complete idiot to spoil the evening with a heart-to-heart discussion about Carl Noble. He wouldn't ask any questions and she wouldn't tell any well-meaning lies to avoid hurting his feelings.

"Carl was an important part of my life."

"*Was* is the operative word, Caroline. I don't mean to be heartless or cruel, but your husband is dead and buried. Let's leave him that way."

"Is that how you feel? That ignorance is bliss?"

"Damned straight, it is." With his eyes on Caroline he eased the truck forward as the car in front of him moved.

"You won't throw your allegation that I'm a gold digger in my face?"

"For Pete's sake, Caroline." His voice raised in volume for emphasis. "I swear on a stack of Bibles ten feet high that those two words, *gold* and *digger,* have been stricken from my vocabulary! Okay?"

"How about country-fried chicken and peach cobbler?" Gilda asked, a mile-wide grin on her mouth. "Are they still in your vocabulary?"

Caroline slid down in her seat wishing she could slide under it. She'd been so single-mindedly intent on ferreting out information from Lee that she hadn't paid attention to where they were. The few people in town who hadn't heard Lee shouting "gold digger" would be getting it secondhand within the next five minutes.

Tongue-tied, Lee could only nod at Gilda, then sheepishly glance at Caroline. Her face seemed to glow in the dark. Her embarrassment made him want to cut out his tongue.

"Good to see the two of you back together," Gilda remarked, hanging halfway out the window to make certain she didn't miss Caroline's response. When no response was forthcoming, she flicked the micro-

phone situated on her flat chest and said loudly,
"Guess I'll have to phone Sadie and offer her a re-
fund on the peach cobbler I sent out to the Carson
place."

"Don't bother with the phone," Caroline muttered. "I'm sure she heard you and Lee."

"What'd you say, sweetie?"

"I said, I'll have corn on the bone," Caroline
quickly replied. "So will Lee."

Chuckling, Gilda repeated, "Corn on the bone.
Sweet land of mercy, it's been a long time since I've
heard you kids call corn on the cob by its nickname."

While Gilda turned back and shouted the order to
J.W., Lee silently composed an apology. *I'm sorry*
seemed puny, and yet he must have whispered his
thoughts aloud because he heard an apology.

"I'm sorry," Caroline restated quietly when Lee
continued to stare blindly through the windshield.
While she apologized, she tried to think of something
to stop Gilda from spreading a choice tidbit of gossip. "It was my fault."

"Hardly. I was the one doing the shouting."

"I provoked you." Caroline worried her bottom lip
with her teeth, then admitted, "Carl often scolded me
for being provocative."

Lee ignored the pinprick of pain caused by the affection he heard in her voice when she mentioned her
husband by name.

"Honey, I'm the one who should be apologizing to
you." He glanced at the vacant drive-up window before saying, "Call it jealousy, possessiveness . . . hell,
a little obsessiveness, I suppose. I don't know how to
explain it other than your marrying Carl wasn't part
of the overall grand scheme I'd planned for us."

"Shh. Here she comes," Caroline warned. "Play along with anything I say, okay?" In a louder voice, she said, "I'm aware you're an expert when it comes to real estate, but do you really believe those wild rumors about gold being panned out of the Intracoastal Waterway?"

"I swore I wouldn't talk about it anymore." He zipped his finger across his mouth. "My lips are sealed."

"It's ridiculous. Gold? In Georgia?" She dropped her voice to a whisper. "Even if a few flakes of gold were found, I wouldn't risk the Noble money buying stock in a gold-digging operation."

"Mining," Lee corrected, winking at Caroline. He admired the agile workings of her clever mind. Everything she said neatly fit the oath he made that Gilda had overheard.

"You can't talk me into it. Starting up the mill is a risky venture. I don't care if the people who contacted you find fist-sized nuggets." Caroline had great difficulty keeping a straight face when Gilda lost her balance and almost fell through the window. "No one can lure me with the glitter of gold. Let somebody else dig for it."

"Did I hear you mention somebody digging for gold?" Gilda asked.

"It's nothing, Gilda," Lee said swiftly. "Just a crackpot rumor. We were just fooling around."

Gilda handed Lee two brown paper sacks, then glanced at the plain gold band on her ring finger. "I always wanted me a chunk of gold. Couple of years back, J.W. and me did a little panning out in California. Didn't find nothing, but..." A dreamy expression crossed her face. "I'd sure like to give it another whirl."

"I'm telling you like it is, Gilda. There is no gold in Georgia. It's pure speculation." Caroline shook her finger at Gilda. "Don't you succumb to gold fever like Lee has. You've got your own gold mine right here in Graceville."

"I reckon you're right, but…gold…practically at my doorstep." She bent toward Lee and whispered, "Do you have a map?"

"No. No gold."

Gilda thoughtfully tapped her chin. "J.W. and me can't get over there until Monday 'cause of the business and all."

"I'd appreciate it if you'd keep quiet about this," Lee said, knowing that saying this guaranteed the rumor would circulate faster than wildfire in a dry marsh. "Just in case you do decide to take a…*fishing trip*… you wouldn't want all the fish gone before you get there."

"Gotcha. You wouldn't mind me sharing the *fish* with a couple of folks, would you?"

"Nobody," Lee and Caroline chorused.

Eager to get out of town before Lee spoiled their cover-up story by doubling over in a fit of laughter, Caroline said, "See you, Gilda."

"Yeah, see you!" Lee echoed. The laughter that had been rumbling in his chest burst free as he pulled from the drive-up window. "You were fantastic! I lost track of how many times you told Gilda there wasn't a word of truth in anything she'd overheard. The more you insisted it was a lie, the more Gilda believed it to be the gospel truth!"

"What about you and your don't-you-tell-anybody routine? I'll bet every business located on the town's square will have Gone Fishing signs on their locked doors. Aren't you ashamed of yourself?"

"Nope," Lee replied smugly. "What about you?"

"I'm feeling no shame, either. Sunshine and salt air will be much better for their mental health than sitting at Gilda's soaking up the latest gossip."

"Amen!"

Seven

"It isn't like Whispering Oaks," Caroline commented as Lee pulled up the lane in front of his house. Landscaping floodlights lit the gray exterior walls, and the lush plants nestled against them. "It's very contemporary."

Lee studied her face, wanting to get an insight into her thoughts. She was comparing his home to Whispering Oaks. He'd probably made similar comparisons the first day he'd gone over the plans with the architect: a traditional Georgian plantation home, two-story, brick, with wide verandas and ornate pillars versus a multilevel, wooden structure, with small balconies jutting from each room.

He'd broken away from his early concept of what was pleasing to his eyes when the architect had explained the advantages of living in a technological "smart house."

He sat quietly, hoping and praying Caroline approved of his choice when he could have been using his persuasive powers to sway her opinion. His home had won various awards and been featured in a recent issue of *Architectural Digest*. But those professional accolades were less meaningful to him than her opinion.

The longer she remained mute, the tighter the muscles across his shoulders grew. Had Justin been right for once in his life? Did she hate it? Should he have stuck to the old tried-and-true version of what had curb appeal?

Unable to sit still any longer, he grabbed the two sacks of food and got out of the truck. Like most successful land developers, he began mapping a worst-case scenario: she hates the isolated location and the contemporary design.

So what?

Lee realized he was letting his old feelings for Caroline—ones she hadn't shared—inflate the value of her giving his home a stamp of approval.

Caroline scrambled out of her seat when Lee slammed his door. The second her foot touched the walkway leading to the front door a river of small lights lit the path. Delighted, feeling like an adventuresome Goldilocks, she dashed toward the front door calling back to Lee, "Come on, slowpoke! I'm anxious to see the inside!"

"It isn't formal." Like Whispering Oaks, he cautioned, lengthening his stride to catch up with her.

The porch light flicked on when Caroline bounced up the steps. No one locked their doors in Graceville so she automatically reached for the knob. Her hand grabbed at thin air. Perplexed, she glared at the smooth surface. "There's no doorknob?"

"The entire house is computerized." He placed his thumb on a small button located beneath a pad of digital numbers. The door swung open. "I could have chosen the voice-activated version, but . . ."

Caroline scooted inside while Lee continued his high-tech explanation. She'd read about computerized homes, but those articles hadn't prepared her for the cornucopia of sensations that actually being in one caused.

Her eyes were drawn to the soaring wall of glass overlooking the Intracoastal Waterway, fell to the informal clusters of cream-colored leather furniture and landed on the plush carpet, which beckoned her to kick off her sandals and get a real feel for casual elegance.

"It's . . . stunning," she gasped, smiling up at Lee. Her eyes sparkled with excitement. Thinking more of Lee's accomplishments than the house, she added, "Absolutely magnificent!"

Mentally prepared for the worst, Lee momentarily had difficulty accepting her praise. "You don't care that it's nothing like Whispering Oaks."

"Nope." She relieved him of the two flattened sacks he'd crushed against his chest. They were a good excuse to investigate the kitchen area. "I'd say your home is strictly Lee Carson—bold, futuristic, yet with a steady eye focused on creature comforts. Where's the kitchen?"

Elated by her compliments, Lee found himself speechless for the second time in less than an hour. He pointed behind her, to the left.

"Practical, too," Caroline noted as she followed the tile walkway until she reached three steps that led to another open area.

Although this one was considerably smaller than the living area, Lee had kept the feel of spaciousness. As she opened the sacks on the curved counter that separated the kitchen from the dinette, she noted he'd equipped the kitchen with the latest in appliances.

"Why don't you wander around and make yourself at home while I heat up dinner?" Lee offered. He picked up the container, grimaced as he noticed the caved-in plastic foam packaging and crossed to the microwave oven. "I'll give a shout when it's ready."

"A shout? No space-age intercom system? No robotic version of an English butler announcing dinner?" she teased blithely.

Her hand moved to her heart; it swelled with pride as she watched him. Lee Carson had beaten the odds stacked up against him. He'd never had a home he could call his own. Abandoned on the doorsteps of Whispering Oaks by his mother when he was only a tiny baby, he'd been shuffled from one foster home to another at the whim of the man he couldn't even legitimately call father. He'd endured the snickers and hurtful remarks his illegitimacy had caused. A lesser man would have hung his head in shame and amounted to nothing.

Lee had risen above his mother's disgrace. He'd grown straight and tall, not to mention sexy as sin, she mused. Other than for sentimental reasons, she couldn't understand why he'd want Whispering Oaks. This house was a tribute to his hard work and ingenuity.

It was no wonder he'd gained respect in Graceville. She thought her heart would burst with pride.

"No robots. I passed on that option. I'm waiting for the wind-current system." He glanced at her as he filled a glass with ice by pressing a lever on the refrigerator door. He put down the glass and spread his arms wide. "It's supposed to envelop a gorgeous woman in a sea breeze and guide her straight into the homeowner's open arms."

A gentle hint was all the encouragement Caroline needed to move across the kitchen. She wound her arms around his waist, nestled her head on his chest and had the distinct feeling of finally coming home.

"Do you truly like it?" Lee whispered, still unsure and vulnerable where she was concerned.

"I love it." Her arms tightened around him when she felt his lips brush against her hair.

Her straightforward reply bolstered his confidence. His fears that his home wouldn't measure up to her dream house began to abate. "What about Whispering Oaks?"

"Are you asking me if I still want it?" She rocked back in the cradle of his arms to be able to see his face. The timer on the microwave dinged, but she ignored it when he nodded. "Whispering Oaks has been the magical kingdom in my fantasies for as long as I can remember. It's ingrained in me that anyone who lives there will live happily ever after. I know that's pure foolishness...as silly as Gilda believing she'd be happy wearing a gold nugget ring."

She thought Lee would smile when she mentioned the prank they'd pulled. He didn't. The way his hands slid restlessly up and down her back was the only indication that he'd heard her.

"Realistically speaking," she continued, "I'm aware that ownership of Whispering Oaks...or Mother's farm...or even the mill, won't buy me happiness. I can honestly say I'm feeling much happier right now than I did when Regina handed me the bill of sale on the mill."

"You're happy here?" His voice broke, but with her cradled in his arms he was unable to mask his emotions. His heart hammered faster than the nail gun that had been used to frame his house. Lee pushed a deep breath out of his lungs in an effort to slow the surge of hot blood pumping through his veins.

"Yes."

She looked up at him and found him gazing down at her with grave intensity. Her stomach tightened in anticipation when a hint of a smile sent lines radiating around his eyes. She knew she should say something to break the mesmerizing effect he had on her, but she lacked the will.

His fingertips moved up her back, lingered at her nape, then lightly caressed the curve of her earlobe. Her pulse raced beneath the light, tender touch of his thumb as his hand settled on her throat. His other hand settled on her hip, drawing her tightly against him.

She could read the hunger and yearning in his eyes. It was as though in their gray depths she could see the fleeting moments of passion they'd shared on the lane that led to Whispering Oaks. There was a volatile chemistry between them, and yet, he seemed reluctant to resume where they'd left off. He appeared to be fighting some imaginary battle in his mind.

"Lee?" She raised her hand to the side of his face. "What's wrong?"

"Nothing." Everything. He wanted her so badly he could taste the honeyed-spice flavor of her mouth without kissing her. He could barely think about anything except the feel of her lips, the supple texture of her skin, the way her nipples had puckered into tight rosebuds beneath his touch.

He should never have touched her. He'd pay dearly for those memories. Later, when she was gone, he knew he'd be staring into the darkness, missing her, wanting her, and knowing she'd never be his. She'd left him once because he'd had nothing to offer her. Knowing he had nothing to offer her now that she didn't already have made a sinking sensation settle in the pit of his stomach.

"That's what you always used to say. Talk to me, Lee," she urged. "Don't treat me like I'm still a little kid."

"You aren't a kid. That *is* the problem." While his eyes dropped to the swell of her breasts and his hand rose from her hip to span the width of her narrow waist, he struggled to find a retort that would spark her temper. Her anger was his only defense. "I can't swat you on the fanny and tell you to buzz off when you start bothering me, can I?"

"Is that what you want?" Afraid she'd misread what she'd seen in his eyes as wishful thinking on her part, she lowered her hand to his chest to push away from him. "Am I a bother?"

The unexpected sight of moisture shimmering in Caroline's eyes unraveled Lee's intent to pick a fight. Compulsively his arms circled her, lifting her off her feet, diminishing their difference in height.

"Yeah, you bother the hell out of me," he confessed hoarsely. His mouth began hungrily devouring her lips. Between hard wet kisses, he whispered, "What I want is you, Caroline. Here. In *my* house. Now."

The persuasive demands of his lips prevented her from either consenting or rejecting him. With her feet off the floor and her head spinning from his kisses, she couldn't think, much less talk. The crushing hold she had on him made breathing difficult.

Truth be told, she didn't give a damn about doing any one of the three, especially talking. When they talked, they fought. She wanted a heated exchange between them, but just this once, she didn't want it to be a verbal one.

Breathing harshly, Lee held on to Caroline, expecting her to wiggle out of his arms, hurl a sassy comment at him and then sashay out the front door. The realization that her arms were looped around his neck, her fingers making dents in the muscles of his back, caused his knees to threaten to buckle beneath him.

"Is this okay with you?" he asked huskily.

A hint of a smile curved her thoroughly kissed lips. Big, tough Lee Carson—the man who'd taken on Graceville single-handedly and won. And yet when it came to making love to her, he sought approval.

"It's more than okay. It's what's right for both of us."

Lee made no attempt to conceal the effect she had on him as he loosened his arms and let her slowly slide down his body until her feet touched the floor. "You're sure?"

"Love me, Lee. For tonight we'll pretend I never climbed aboard that bus to Atlanta."

"I would have married you that day." He turned her until she fit neatly under his arm with her flushed cheek against his chest. Slowly, giving her an opportunity to change her mind, he moved toward the master bedroom.

"I know you would have."

"And somehow I'd have given you everything your heart desired."

"I only have one desire tonight, Lee." She hugged his waist as he opened the door to his room. "You."

He swept her into his arms to carry her across the threshold. His mouth caught hers as he mentally turned back the pages to the day after her eighteenth birthday. The same judge who auctioned off the mill would have married them. He imagined them, standing hand in hand. Scared and defiant. Unsure, and yet determined. They'd have found a place, any place, and he'd have carried her across the threshold just as he'd carried her into his bedroom tonight.

He crossed to the wide bed. With a flick of his wrist he pulled back the quilted coverlet before he lowered Caroline to the bed's edge. He would have knelt before her to remove her shoes, but she lithely kicked off the gold-toned flats. Her arms drew him down beside her.

Slowly, thoroughly, he took possession of her mouth once more. His fingers unbuttoned the tiny cloth-covered buttons, ones much like those on a fancy wedding dress. With reverence, he parted the shimmering gold material. His knuckles scooted across the lacy edge of her bra until he felt its clasp. He flicked it undone. And still he kissed her, rhythmically rubbing his tongue against hers.

Caroline shrugged out of the top half of her jumpsuit and her bra while his hands caressed elongated

circles from her shoulders to her waist, deftly assist-
ing her in removing the frothy piece of lace.

His gray eyes appeared black and brilliant when he
looked at her. Without saying anything, he made her
feel as though the fresh dew of youth still clung to her
skin. Being unclothed to the waist in front of a man
was new to her. And yet, because it was Lee appreciatively gazing at her, she forgot that she had never given
herself in this way before.

"You're so beautiful," he whispered, his voice thick
with unbridled passion. His hand covered her breast,
kneading it until her pinkish-brown nipples pearled in
his palm.

Wanting to return the pleasurable feelings, Caroline let her fingers score a path up the tense muscles of
his back. When she felt his tension ebbing, her hands
moved to the front of his shirt. She wasn't as dexter-
ous as he'd been, but he didn't seem to notice.

The bed shifted as he stripped off his shirt in one
fluid motion. He wanted to bring her nipples to life
between his tongue and the roof of his mouth. He
didn't though. Slowly, oh so slowly, he lowered his
chest to cover hers. He felt her breasts pucker into
tight buds when they touched his furred chest. Her
gasp made him want the ecstasy to last forever.

"Oh yes, sweetheart," he sighed as the imaginary
line between ecstasy and torment became as thin as the
edge of a razor.

"Did I hurt you?" Caroline asked, her voice filled
with concern as she moved her knees away from the
juncture of his thighs. She must have, she decided,
concerned by the pained expression on his face. She
levered her arms between them and attempted to move

to his side, but his hands settled firmly on her hips to prevent her.

"No." Lee sent a silent prayer heavenward: Don't let me louse this up, Lord. One misspoken word, one clumsy movement on his part could make the difference between heaven and hell.

"Then what's wrong? Did my belt buckle scratch you?" Caroline sat up higher, her toes curled under his thighs to keep her balance. One hand swept across his abdomen as the other hand mopped her hair back from her face. "There's no red mark."

His stomach muscles quivered beneath her fingers. His fingers tightened on the curve of her hips to prevent her from moving away from him. "Caroline...Caroline...Caroline," he chanted, lifting his shoulders off the pillows until he'd folded her securely into his arms. He held her fiercely and whispered, "This is a dream. I'm afraid I'm going to wake up and discover the past two days were a figment of my imagination."

Caroline swayed against him. She felt a renewed desire to give him pleasure. And just because she was inexperienced didn't mean she was ignorant. She'd watched movies and television; she'd read romances. She had strong notions as to what sexually excited a man. That knowledge, along with the confidence of knowing how much Lee wanted her, liberated her inhibitions.

Still astride him, with her thighs clamped against his narrow hips, she circled against him. He caved backward against the pillows, his hips arched. She felt the hard ridge of his manhood thrust against her through the double layer of material, his trousers and her jumpsuit. She wasn't shocked or mortified by his instantaneous response, or her own. Her body seemed to liquefy at the sweet, wild intimacy.

She caught her lower lip between her teeth when he began peppering hot moist kisses on her breasts. And when he pulled her nipple into his mouth, a spasm of intense pleasure ricocheted through her. She clung to him. With each suckling movement of his lips and tongue she felt drawn deeper and deeper into the hot vortex of his mouth.

Her eyelids felt heavy, weighted, too heavy to keep open. He caressed and fondled her; she pressed and rotated against the strength of his arousal.

She was so lost in the myriad of sensations he created she wasn't aware of his left hand unbuckling her wide belt or the sound of her zipper being lowered. She had no more will than a fragile piece of Chantilly lace when he lifted her and removed her garment. He dropped her jumpsuit off the edge of the bed. Within seconds his slacks and briefs lay beside the liquid gold fabric puddled on the carpet.

The imaginary patterns she traced on his chest, shoulders and arms were erratic, fashioned in a design that would elicit low throaty growls of approval from Lee. She had no master pattern. Only her feminine instincts guided her as she curled her fingers around him. She hesitated, momentarily glorying in the power she felt as she heard him gasp for air.

She forced her eyes open, wanting to see him, then went weak and soft when she saw how the dark centers of his eyes seemed to have expanded until the grayness had disappeared. Passion had carved deep lines along his cheeks. His tanned skin appeared tautly stretched across his cheekbones.

And then his hand drifted lazily below her navel. Caroline cried out as the ache that wound inside her threatened to explode. He touched her, there, at the dewy source of her pulsating desire. She rose higher on her knees to give him free access.

"Wild. Sexy. Passionate. Not a wild child, but a wildly passionate woman," he praised, gently parting her soft folds of flesh, his finger erotically stroking her. When she imitated his rhythmic stroking with her hand, he feared his silent vow to take this slow and easy would be broken. His entire body throbbed. He wrapped his arm around her waist and sexily demanded, "Move beside me on the bed."

Her initial awkwardness vanished as she gracefully followed his command. Settling her against him, he whispered his intentions. Her muscles involuntarily tensed in anticipation. She felt like a length of thread being tightly wound. At any moment she expected the tension coiling deep inside of her to snap and unravel. Even though she was far less experienced than anybody knew, she was beyond caring about the possibility of minor pain. Nothing worthwhile had ever been easy for her.

From what seemed a million miles away, she heard the rustle of foil. Once, aeons ago, she'd refused Lee's proposals because she had feared making an innocent child part of the cycle of poverty. Although they'd both broken the cycle, she realized he still wanted to protect her.

"No babies," he whispered. "Not until you want them."

His motives for protecting Caroline were not entirely unselfish. He had his own hellish demons to contend with, too. No one would call any child of his a bastard.

When he moved between Caroline's legs, their eyes met and held, hers filled with unspoken questions, his holding all the answers. There was nothing for her to be afraid of, nothing for her to run away from. He'd take care of her as he'd always promised to do.

Her eyes widened as he sank into her. She could feel the narrow passage stretch to adjust to him. The expression on Lee's face made him look as though he were the one in pain. Did ecstasy and pain wear the same mask? She had her answer when she felt him slowly withdraw. It wasn't ecstasy she'd seen. It was Lee exercising extreme control.

She locked her legs around his waist and arched her hips, taking full responsibility for the consequences of her actions as he deeply penetrated her. She gradually relaxed when he resided deep within her. His head had dropped to her chest; his elbows supported his weight. Prompted by a primitive longing, she rotated her hips beneath him.

Unable to separate reality from his fantasy of being her first lover, Lee squeezed his eyes shut until vibrantly colored spots floated in the total darkness. A married woman can't be a virgin, he told himself silently. But he could have sworn he'd been the first to breach the thin barrier of her femininity. His imagination had played dozens of tricks on him before tonight where Caroline was concerned, but none of them had seemed this real!

He opened his eyes and lifted his face until their eyes locked. Caroline felt her heart swell. It should have been her eyes that were filling with tears. It wasn't. Only his dark eyes glistened with moisture.

Intuitively she knew the difficult part was behind her. In the full sense of the word, she was a woman.

With her thumb, she wiped away the lonesome tear that trickled down his cheek. She hugged him, clinging with her arms and legs, rocking against the strength and length of him. With each parry and thrust, each one harder and faster, she whispered, "Yes, Lee, oh, yes."

In a frenzy of pleasure, Lee whispered love words, words of encouragement and praise. Caroline felt as though her climb up the ladder of success was merely a small step in the right direction compared to how Lee made her feel. She felt dizzy from the height, as though she'd explode from the pressure building within her.

And then, with one heart-wrenching thrust, he lifted her higher until she reached the pinnacle of her heart's desire. She shouted his name, not in anger, but in glorious rapture.

Later, lying close to him, Lee watched a lifetime of repressed tears sliding across her cheeks. Only the smug smile curving her love-swollen lips relieved his mind of worry. In order to give her the moments of solitude she needed, he crossed to the bathroom to wash up. When he returned, she'd wiped away all traces of her tears, leaving only the smug smile. She was feeling proud of herself and didn't mind showing it.

Lee snuggled up next to her and asked an age-old question, "Was it good for you?"

She nodded and grinned.

Feeling ten feet tall and strong as a lumberjack, Lee rewarded her with a hug. "Dare I ask how good?"

"I am not going to rate making love to you on a scale of one to ten," she replied with a grin.

"C'mon, Caroline. You're as smug as a realtor who closes a million-dollar deal the same day he passed the realty exam. Turnabout is fair play. Make me smug, too. Feed my ego," he teased. When she raised one eyebrow, silently demanding to know what he meant, he added, "Your feeding my ego will be a rare experience for me."

Glad Lee wasn't one of those men she'd read about in the women's magazines, the ones who rolled over and snored after making love, Caroline was only too willing to pillow talk.

"A smug realtor, hmm?" She chuckled and skittered her fingers across his chest, over the gold herringbone necklace he wore, to his broad shoulder. Pretending to contemplate his request she twisted the gold chain around her index finger. "You make me feel the way I did the first time I sewed a collar to a shirt that didn't get tossed in the pile of seconds."

"You felt that good, huh?"

"Better, actually."

"How much better?"

"Would you believe . . . better than putting the perfect rolled hem in multiple layers of chiffon?" She looped another length of his chain around her finger until it tightened like a noose around his neck. "You're the perfect buttonhole, the perfect-fitting pants, the perfect-tailored suit . . ."

"Perfect?" Lee crowed, growing another inch or two in stature.

Caroline nodded and dropped the necklace back in place. She would have demanded an equal amount of praise, but a low rumble coming from under the sheet brought a burst of laughter from Lee.

"What was it your etiquette book said about growling stomachs? What page?" he teased, tweaking her chin between his thumb and forefinger. "And isn't that a no-no?"

Caroline gave him a wide-eyed innocent look and confessed glibly, "That was pure fabrication on my part. I don't own any such book."

"Good. I'd rather have you be what you are by nature—one hell of a woman—not an uptight, prim and proper lady. How do you feel about eating chicken with your fingers?"

As though on cue, her stomach answered for her.

"There's a robe hanging on the door in the bathroom. Why don't you slip into it while I go down and warm up dinner?" As he whisked back the sheet and watched her leave his bed and cross the room, a replica of her smug smile curved the corners of his mouth.

The way Caroline made him feel, he wanted to spread rose petals in front of her feet, to wrap her in diamonds and furs, to give her things no other man could give her.

Lee's thoughts reversed in time, back to the courthouse parking lot. In anger he'd yelled, *I have something you want that can't be bought with a dead man's gold.* His mind jumped to Gilda's Café, where Caroline had quizzed the banker about the Jackson farm.

He did have something she treasured—a quitclaim deed to her mother's farm. He'd wanted to tell her he'd been the one to give Hector the hundred-dollar bills, but he'd been sidetracked by Caroline's determination to go to Whispering Oaks.

Grinning, he bounded off the bed, stooped to pick up his slacks and strode into the sitting room, which adjoined the master bedroom. Seconds later, he was zipping up his pants as he removed the deed from his safe. His fingertips slid over the smooth satin surface of the red ribbon he'd tied around it so many years ago.

"She's mine now, Carl Noble," he mouthed silently. Lee gritted his teeth as he pushed back the painful memories crowding into his mind. "I can forget her past. I have to!"

Eight

Out of habit, Caroline made a quick inventory of her appearance in the full-length mirrors in Lee's bathroom as she attempted to knot his terry-cloth robe at her waist. "It's...roomy," she said, grinning at the reflection of a pint-size woman in a ten-gallon-size robe.

Deciding his robe was too big for comfort or appeal—two of the factors that had made the CJN label in designer clothes popular—she shrugged out of it and crossed into the bedroom to retrieve her jumpsuit. Without inspecting the garment, she slipped into it, unconsciously confident the fabric she'd chosen would be wrinkle-free.

As she buttoned the top of her jumpsuit, her eyes appreciatively roamed around the carved oak furniture in Lee's bedroom, pausing when they reached the rumpled bed linens. She noticed a tiny smear of blood on the bottom sheet. Her brow wrinkled as she wondered why Lee hadn't made mention of her virginity.

Wasn't being a woman's first lover supposed to be important to a man?

She stopped frowning, realizing she was glad Lee hadn't made a big deal out of it. Carl had his share of male pride and a strong sense of cautiousness. No one knew they had slept in separate bedrooms. He didn't want to take any chance of their not consummating their wedding vows becoming a weapon for his relatives to use against her in court. A discussion with Lee about her husband's inability to have sex would have left her feeling as though she'd betrayed Carl's confidence.

She pulled up the top sheet, then stopped when she noticed the paper bound with a red ribbon lying on the pillow.

A love note?

Caroline smiled. Picking up the paper, she momentarily held it against her heart before sitting on the edge of the bed and untying the ribbon. Such a sweetheart, she thought as she unfolded the note. Such a sensitive man.

"Such a...*paid in full!*" She gasped in shock, reading the large red letters stamped across the top of the document. Her eyes narrowed as she scanned the contents of the quitclaim deed to the Jackson farm signed by her uncle and Lee. Instantly she put two and two together and came up with the person who'd given Hector the wad of hundred-dollar bills big enough to choke a horse.

Caroline made a choking sound. Her hands clenched the paper into a tight ball. A mental picture of the bitter expression on Lee's face as he'd called her a gold digger formed in her mind.

Don't get mad, get even. That's what he believes.

She couldn't think of a more despicable way for him to get his revenge for her buying the Carson Mill than making love to her, then leaving the equivalent of a wad of money on her pillow!

No wonder he hadn't asked about being the first man she'd slept with.

She shuddered, remembering how she'd fed his ego by telling him how wonderful their lovemaking had been. Silently she cursed herself for being so love-starved, so easily duped, so damned naive. Ashamed of herself, she shoved Lee's "love note" under the pillow, wishing she'd never returned to Graceville.

She'd told herself to be wary of him. Why hadn't she listened to her own good advice?

Caroline bounced to her feet, too agitated to remain seated. The urge to flee from a bad situation lengthened her stride as she traveled through the hall leading to the kitchen.

"Gold is definitely your color," Lee commented, noticing how the fabric brought out the reddish highlights of her hair and the flushed pinkness of her cheeks. "Ready to have some chicken and cobbler?"

"No." She made a sharp left toward the front door without a pause. "I've already been bought and paid for. You don't have to feed me."

"What?"

Caroline had no inclination to pander to Lee by stopping to explain. Let him play innocent to some other woman, she thought. As far as she was concerned he was about as innocent as a shyster selling swampland to little old ladies. Well, he'd underestimated her. She didn't have to be knee-deep in muck to know she'd made a bad mistake.

"You can't leave now!" Lee shouted, frustrated by her complete flip-flop in temperament.

"Slither out from under your rock and watch me."

Having reached the front door, she glanced over her shoulder as she grabbed for the doorknob. Lee wasn't in sight, but she could hear him coming toward her. Her hand clenched into an empty fist where the knob should have been. Spotting the pad of buttons on the wall, she began poking them. Music started to play and the blinds closed. She jabbed another series of buttons. The chandelier blinked on and off. Lights in the living room came on. And finally, the door opened.

"You aren't going anywhere!"

She dashed toward Lee's truck. The hell she wasn't. She couldn't get off his property fast enough. Fortunately the tailgate was unlocked. If it hadn't been, Caroline felt certain that with the amount of adrenaline pumping through her at its present rate, she could have ripped off the handle. The moped seemed as light as a piece of chiffon as she hoisted it to the ground.

"Dammit, Caroline! What put a bee in your bonnet?" Lee jogged down the path to the driveway. "Wait a minute, would you?"

"You paid what you thought I was worth." Her eyes angrily sliced through the darkness as she straddled the moped. The slight discomfort caused when she landed on the leather seat stoked the fires of her outrage. The engine roared. Shouting over it, she yelled, "Did you expect me to spend the whole night for a few hundred dollars?"

Lee grabbed her wrists and manacled them together in one hand. "I didn't make that deal with
Hector because I wanted a quick roll in the hay. I made
it to prove I could give you anything your heart desired!"

"Don't lie to me. There's a hole in that story big
enough to drive an eighteen-wheel truck through!"

"I'm not lying! Did you see the date on it? Back
then I had it all worked out in my mind. I'd stride into
the department store where Jimbo told me you
worked. I'd present you with the quitclaim deed and
you'd fall into my arms. Then I'd bring you back to
Graceville, you'd marry me, and we'd live happily ever
after."

"You never came to Atlanta!"

"The hell I didn't. I made a complete fool of myself over you! The saleslady led me to the designers'
salon and began showing me dresses with your label in
them. Dammit, I was actually proud of you for making it on your own until she kicked the slats out from
under me by telling me you'd married the boss! You
were on your honeymoon!"

"Don't expect me to believe that cock-and-bull
story. You're just trying to lay a guilt trip on me for
not dropping you a postcard! Jimbo would have told
me if you'd gone to Atlanta!"

"Not unless he wanted to permanently limp on both
legs! I came back to Graceville and threatened to break
both of Jimbo's legs if he ever mentioned your name
to me or my name to you! Then I locked the deed in
the safe and swore I'd cut out my tongue before I'd
ever speak your name again!"

"I wish you *had* cut it out!" She tried to land a jab
with one elbow, but Lee straightened his arms in the

nick of time. "I'd have cut it out myself if I'd known how you were going to use it to sweet-talk yourself into getting even with me!"

"I swear, Caroline Jackson, there are times when you're more trouble than you're worth!" he yelled, totally exasperated with her. "So help me, you're pushing me to the point where I could cheerfully throttle you without feeling an ounce of remorse!"

Caroline jerked downward and freed her hands. The momentum of her swing knocked Lee off balance. He grabbed for the handlebars but missed. Intent on getting far away as quickly as possible, she squeezed the throttle.

The wheels of the moped rolled forward. The lump she felt under the front tire could have been a rock or it could have been Lee's toes. She heard him bellow a curse word and wished the tire tracks on his toes were straight up the middle of his chest!

Then we'd be even, she silently blasted, feeling as though he'd trampled on her heart.

Hunkered low over the handlebars to decrease the wind resistance, she sped out of his drive and down the lane.

I'll never trust him again, she vowed. Thoroughly humiliated, she pushed the moped to the limits of its power. It would be just like Lee to chase after her, trying to get the last word. She glanced in her side mirror. Several hundred yards behind her, twin beams of headlights were creeping up behind her moped.

Her first impulse was to pull off the road and give him holy hell, but she quickly decided she'd be wiser to stick her nose in the air and pretend she didn't notice him.

How could she not notice him when his engine was practically warming her backside?

He kept pace, slowly edging closer and closer. His bright lights blinded her when she glanced in her side mirror.

"Get off my tail, Lee Carson!"

She raised her left arm and motioned for him to stop tailgating. She felt as though she'd been swallowed by the lights as the truck's high beams stretched out farther in front of her than her own light. Much closer and her moped would be an ornament on the hood of his truck!

Abruptly her instinct for self-preservation began sending warning signals. *I could cheerfully throttle you,* she heard him say again. *Without remorse.* Was cheerfully throttling the same as playing bumper tag?

The thought chilled her to the bone. Lee Carson wouldn't be the first man obsessed by a woman who scorned him. He wouldn't be the first to resort to violence, either. What if he wanted to get rid of her?

She had no idea how far she'd traveled or how much farther it was to town. She began to frantically search for a side road. Even a wide place in the narrow two-lane road would do. What the moped lacked in speed had to be made up for in agility.

There's one, she silently screamed, spying a dirt road that forked off sharply to the left. She couldn't slow down for fear of being run over. All she could do was hang on and hope and pray she wouldn't flip when she made the turn.

You aren't going to get me, she swore between clenched teeth. You aren't going to get me!

She swerved left. Her back wheel lost traction as it left the blacktop road and hit the sand. Caroline instantly loosened her hand on the throttle. The impact of the rush of air blowing off the truck as it whizzed by her added to her difficulties.

For several seconds she fought to keep the moped in an upright position. The rear wheel swerved in one direction, then the other. Caroline felt as though her arms would be wrenched from their sockets as she valiantly struggled to counter the pull of the terrain. Finally, she rolled to a stop.

Breathing heavily, her legs feeling like elastic, she slumped over the handlebars. She had enough presence of mind to peer down the road in an effort to get a license plate number, but whoever was driving the truck had turned off his lights. All she could see was a dark object rapidly disappearing from sight.

A shiver of aftershock coursed through her. She'd been so certain Lee was her friend. She'd halfway convinced herself that she loved him. "Oh, Lee," she gasped, scared out of her mind, "you almost paid my fare for a one-way ticket out of here!"

Her false sense of security combined with her independent streak had made her an easy target.

"No more," she vowed, chafing her arms as goose bumps sprinkled across her skin. Tomorrow, first thing, she'd make arrangements for a car. A big, heavy car, she corrected. A Sherman tank would be good.

Right now, she had to concentrate on getting back to town safely. She turned the moped around and edged slowly back to the highway. The thought of Lee's truck parked beside the road waiting to make a second assault sent another chill through her. As she turned left and headed down the road, she kept a sharp eye out. She wasn't going to let anyone get behind her. And if she saw truck lights coming at her, she'd make a dive for the drainage ditch.

Hunched forward, her arms and legs tense, her eyes straining to see into the wall of darkness beyond the range of her headlight, she rode toward town. Her head began to pound. Each swallow she took had the acidic taste of fear. The next seven miles were the longest ones Caroline had ever traveled.

The sight of the motel's neon sign brought a sob of relief through her lips. Two, maybe three blocks, she calculated. She was going to make it!

She nearly fell off her moped when she heard a horn honk at the next side street. Her hand automatically squeezed, goosing the throttle to get across the intersection. A car filled with teenagers, hooting and hollering, crossed over the highway behind her.

"Just a bunch of kids," she said, sighing, slowing down to make the turn into the motel's parking lot.

Caroline made a 360-degree perusal before she parked the moped outside her room. In case someone was watching, she coached herself not to run like a scared rabbit to the safety of her room. Her insides might be shaking like a bowl of gelatin, but she wasn't going to let anyone else know it.

Just as she stuck the key in the lock, she heard the phone ringing inside her room. Slamming the door behind her, she darted to the nightstand and picked up the phone. "Hello?"

"Get outta town," a muffled voice said. "Next time you won't be so lucky. I'm gonna—"

Caroline disconnected the line and pushed the O button. Any call had to come through the switchboard. When the operator answered she demanded,

"A call just came through to room eleven. Can you tell me where it came from?"

"No," a woman replied. "He just asked to be connected to your room. Is there a problem?"

Caroline bit her lip. She could make a big to-do out of this incident and have the operator call the police department, but she decided against it. This was between Lee and her.

"No. No problem. I'd appreciate not having any calls put through after nine o'clock in the evening. Get their names and numbers, though."

"Yes, ma'am. I'll make a note of it. You did have a couple of long distance calls. One from a Regina Parker. She said she'd call back tomorrow."

"I'll take any out-of-town calls. Thanks."

She dropped the phone back to its cradle, then flopped on the bed. Closing her eyes, rubbing her forehead to ease her headache, she made an effort to identify the voice. The caller had disguised it, maybe by putting a handkerchief or a piece of cloth over his mouth. What she'd heard wasn't much louder than a raspy stage whisper.

His message echoed in her mind. *Get out of town. Next time you won't be so lucky... Get out of town... out of town.*

It didn't take a Sherlock Holmes to deduce that the driver of the truck and the caller were the same man.

Lee Carson.

Dawn had barely crept into Caroline's room when she was awake, rubbing her eyes from lack of sleep. She rolled to her side, away from the light. Throughout the night she'd gone over the details of what had happened since she'd returned. She'd readily admitted to having made some mistakes where Lee was concerned. If she could relive her life, she'd have kept in touch with him. Better yet, she'd have realized Lee had cared for her beyond the platonic limitations of friendship. Unintentionally, she'd hurt him.

But any guilt she felt had been eradicated by Lee's behavior. He'd far more than evened the score between them. Lee had made love to her, made her feel alive with pleasure—and then he had paid her off.

Dry-eyed, remembering the tears of joy she'd shed, Caroline ground the heels of her hands into her eye sockets. Realizing she'd spent half the night vilifying Lee and the other half making excuses for him, she vowed to follow the only sensible course of action available. "I'll avoid him. I have plenty to keep me busy. He couldn't make me stay and he can't run me out of town."

She rolled to her back and put her hands behind her head. She'd have to be careful, though. Extremely careful. The first thing she needed to do was take care of her transportation problem.

Following that line of thought, she reached for the phone and dialed Regina's home number.

"Regina?" She'd heard the buzzing tone cease, but nothing had been said. "Are you there?"

"Mmm. Barely."

"You were right about the moped being unsuitable for these roads. I need a truck, something heavy-duty. Any chance of your getting in touch with Tom and having him drive one over today?" Caroline heard Regina doing her best to stifle a yawn. "Regina?"

"Mmm. Are my eyes glued together or is it still dark outside? You'll have to pardon me for not being wide-eyed and bushy-tailed, but it's only..."

Caroline winced as she imagined Regina looking at the clock. It was a bit early for a phone call.

"Six-oh-nine on a Sunday? Lord have mercy, the roosters aren't even crowing this early!" Regina complained. "Why are you calling this early?"

"I wanted to catch you before I went over to Gilda's for breakfast."

"Don't tell me—she's serving worms 'n grits 'n red-eyed gravy for the early birds. Right?"

With a tired grin, Caroline shook her head. "I need a truck," she repeated slowly. "Something heavy-duty. How soon can you get one to Graceville?"

"Could this wait until a decent, respectable hour? Say Monday morning, after nine o'clock?"

"Regina, last night I almost became a red spot on the center line of the highway."

"You what?" Regina gasped.

"You heard me," Caroline said. "Somebody ran me off the road. I don't know if they're trying to frighten me into leaving Graceville or something more permanent, but I don't want to give them an easy target."

"Instead of sending a truck, why doesn't Tom come over with the limo to pick you up and bring you back where you belong?"

"And admit defeat? Uh-uh."

"Did you get a look at the driver...or see the license plate?"

"No."

"Caroline, I don't like this one little bit."

"I can take care of myself. You'd have been proud of me if you'd seen how I whipped the moped onto a side road."

Groaning, Regina said, "I doubt it. I'd probably have fainted. But if you're going to insist on staying in Graceville, why don't I come over there and stay with you?"

"It's not your turn to baby-sit, that's why. I can take care of myself."

"Right," Regina said skeptically.

"You just take care of having Tom deliver the truck. Okay?"

"No, it's not okay, but I can tell you're going to be stubborn about this. I guess there isn't much else you'll let me do for you other than worry, is there?"

"No. I'll be fine," Caroline said, injecting a note of confidence she didn't feel.

"At least you're in a motel where there are other people around. I'd really be worried if you'd bought Whispering Oaks and were staying there."

Caroline couldn't be certain, but she suspected the switchboard operator was a close relative of Gilda's when she heard a tiny gasp of excitement after Regina mentioned Whispering Oaks. She considered feeding the listener another version of the fishing hoax, but decided against it. In the next few days she'd be conducting business via this phone. She had to put a stop to having her calls monitored.

Icicles of authority dripped from her voice when she said, "I suggest whoever is listening in to my private conversation that she gets off the line unless she wants to be waiting tables for her aunt." She felt instant gratification when she heard a click on the line. "Where were we?"

"Whispering Oaks," Regina prompted. "Have you bought it yet?"

"No, but Justin will be glad to hear the rumor the motel switchboard operator will be spreading around about my wanting it."

"I thought you were supposed to have dinner out there. What happened?"

"I met up with an immovable object halfway down the lane. Lee Carson."

"The rip-roaring-mad, illegitimate half brother? Do you think he's the one who tried to splat you on the highway?"

"Maybe," Caroline hedged. Out of habit she had difficulty pointing an accusatory finger in Lee's direction, even when he was the most likely suspect.

"Maybe? Don't you mean probably? When I left he had his hackles raised and you had your claws unsheathed. Frankly, I thought he might have been the one who scratched the limo."

Caroline wasn't about to admit that thought had crossed her mind, too. She couldn't prove anything, but the circumstantial evidence was mounting higher and higher against Lee.

"Caroline? Are you there?"

"Uh-huh. I was wool-gathering." To get Regina off the subject before she started packing her bags to return to Graceville, she added, "I found out why you couldn't locate any liens against the farm."

"Your uncle paid them off?"

"Uh-uh. Lee did. He has a quitclaim deed on the property."

"So where is your Uncle Hector?"

"At the farm. In the papers I read, Lee stipulated that Hector could farm the land—as long as he pays minimum wage to farmhands, and doesn't use child labor."

"Which means that more than likely Hector has to do the work himself or starve. Poetic justice—I love it! Carl would have, too. I hope you drove by the farm and gloated."

"Actually, no. Yesterday was one of those topsy-turvy days. Nothing went as I had planned."

"Are you going out there today?"

"I doubt it." She wasn't going anywhere until she had four wheels under her and armor plate wrapped around her.

Caroline jumped with alarm when someone with heavy fists started banging on her door. Taking the phone with her, she strode toward the window. The cord was too short. She returned the phone to the nightstand. "Somebody's pounding on my door."

"Don't open the door until you know who's on the other side of it!"

"It's probably Jimbo." Another hail of fists slammed against the door. "The phone cord won't reach. I'll talk to you tomorrow, Regina. Bye."

Before Regina could object, Caroline put down the receiver. She crossed to the door, checked the chain lock and cautiously opened the door.

"Take the chain off the door," Lee ordered sternly. "You and I are going to have a long, serious talk."

Caroline started to slam the door, but he wedged his foot in the opening.

"I have nothing to say to you," she said.

"Well I have plenty to say to you!"

"Lower your voice! Do you want to wake up everybody in town?" She ground her bare heel on his toe, knowing it was a puny defensive effort but determined to get the door shut.

"Ouch! That's the toe you ran over last night," Lee said between clenched teeth.

"Is that why you tried to run me down on the highway?" She shifted her weight to the other foot. "To get even?"

"What the hell are you talking about?" Lee roared.

"Somebody—the same somebody who scratched the limo and flattened my tires—tried to run me down. Guess who?"

"Take off the chain, Caroline, or step back. When I bust this door down I don't want you hurt."

"Don't you dare! Do you like making a laughing-stock out of yourself?"

"You're the one who'll have to explain the door hanging from its hinges. You'd better take the chain off."

"No way. I've seen you when you fly off the handle. You can either move your fat foot and back away from the door, or I'll have the sheriff and the fire department here in two seconds flat," she bluffed. "A good spraying down with the water hose ought to cool you off."

Lee lowered his voice to a coaxing whisper. "You know I'd never hurt you."

"Said the fox to the gingerbread boy," she scoffed.

"I just want to talk. You owe me that."

"I don't owe you anything!"

"You do owe me!" he yelled. "The deed was a gift, not payment for—" Lee cringed at the erroneous conclusion she'd drawn "—services rendered."

"For services rendered?" she repeated. What he'd just politely insinuated was worse than calling her a gold digger! "I'm going to count to five, Lee. If I don't see you heading out of the parking lot I won't bother calling the sheriff's department, I'll call the state troopers.''

"Why won't you listen to reason?''

"Another sales pitch is what you mean.'' She began counting, "One . . .''

"I've never lied to you.''

"Two.'' She backed away from the door. "I'm picking up the phone.''

"Dammit, Caroline!''

"Three . . .''

"I didn't try to hurt you. You've got to believe that.''

"Four.''

She sidestepped to the window to see what he was doing. Her traitorous heart skipped a beat when she watched him rake his hands through his dark hair. He looked absolutely adorable unshaved, with his shirt buttoned askew. Her fingers tingled as she remembered how silky his hair had felt. He'd been such a tender, considerate lover—maybe she was wrong. Maybe she'd become ultrasensitive about being considered a gold digger. Maybe he had wanted her to have the farm as a gift. Maybe that hadn't been him on the road. For an instant she gave second thoughts to opening the door.

No! She'd believed the sweet loving lies his silver tongue had spun in his attempt to get even with her. She wasn't going to fall for the same trick twice!

"I'm dialing the number.''

"Okay, Caroline. I'm leaving, but I'll be back.''

"I won't change my mind.'' She saw his mouth move, but couldn't hear what he said. He must have known she was at the window though, because his eyes moved directly to her.

He placed one hand over his heart and the other to his ear, then he pressed his big, callused hand on the window.

Her insides melted as she whispered, "Listen to your heart?" Carl had uttered those same simple words the day he'd died.

Lee nodded.

Tempted to reach out to Lee and put her hand on the other side of the glass, she had to bite her lip to bring her mind back to reality. Lee Carson didn't love her. Every action—almost every action, she amended—showed he hated her. She let the drapes fall from between her fingers, closing the sight of Lee from her eyes.

Nine

"Coffee?" Gilda called, holding up the glass pot. "Two eggs over easy, with a side order of pancakes? Same as Jimbo is having?"

"Yes, please," Caroline answered as she weaved through the tables to the back of the café where her brother was sitting.

The wide grin on Jimbo's face had Caroline worrying how much her brother had learned while he'd been playing detective. Did he know she'd left Justin at Whispering Oaks to be with Lee? Mentally backtracking, she decided he couldn't know. If he'd been following her the near accident wouldn't have happened.

"I saw Lee outside your door when I drove into town, or I'd have picked you up." Jimbo slid off the booth's seat to give Caroline a hug, then asked, "Where is he?"

"He didn't tell me what his plans were for the day."

Caroline noticed Jimbo was looking especially nice in his church clothes—a charcoal gray suit, white shirt, red-and-silver-striped tie. She herself was dressed in skintight turquoise capri pants with an oversize top. The congregation would drop their hymnals if she strode inside the sanctuary. As she sat down and scooted over, she decided that next week she'd make a point of dressing up and going to church with her brother.

Jimbo dropped back onto the seat across from Caroline just as Gilda placed a mug in front of Caroline and began filling it.

"Lee's probably gone fishing," Gilda replied, winking at Caroline.

Looking baffled, Jimbo said, "Fishing? Since when has Lee become a fisherman?"

"Never you mind," Gilda interrupted before Caroline could reply. She gave Jimbo a stern glare as she refilled his cup. "Folks will tell you what they want you to know without you prying information out of them."

"Has she turned over a new leaf?" Jimbo whispered after Gilda had returned to the counter. "Usually she'd blurt out the location of Lee's secret fishing hole and tell what he was using for bait!"

Caroline grinned. "Maybe she's started a new policy. I can't say I'd be distressed if one of the signs over the cash register said No Gossip Allowed."

"Amen!" Jimbo picked up his mug and sipped the hot brew. "So what are your plans for today?"

"I thought I'd start getting my papers organized to take out to the mill tomorrow."

"Sunday is pretty much like any other day of the week when you're self-employed, huh, sis? I guess that's one advantage I have just punching a time clock out at the lumber mill."

"How would you feel about tearing up your time card?"

Jimbo set down his cup. "To work for you?"

"With me," she corrected.

"Where? In Atlanta or here?"

"Here. As office manager at the textile mill." She poured a dollop of cream into her coffee. "I need someone I can trust to take care of business here while I'm in Atlanta hiring jobbers to market our line of fabrics. Eventually Noble Mills will build a reputation that will have the buyers waiting in line outside your office, but that's a few years down the road." She named a salary figure that lit her brother's sky-blue eyes. "Interested?"

Jimbo grinned from ear to ear. "You just hired yourself an office manager."

"You'll be worth every dollar you earn. When can you start?"

"When do you need me?"

"Yesterday," she answered with a smile. "But I'll settle for evenings and weekends until you're available full-time."

"Uh-oh," Jimbo groaned. "Don't look now, but our least favorite relative just walked in the door. He's headed this way."

Reflexively, Caroline braced herself by clamping her fingers around the scalding hot mug. Her chin rose in defiance. It had been years since she'd had an encounter with Hector, but she had to forcefully remind herself that the man had lost the power to browbeat her.

She uncurled her fingers one by one as she turned her head toward the door. She blinked in surprise. She remembered Hector as being a big hulk of a man, at least six feet tall and strong as an ox! Was this stoop-shouldered, emaciated man shuffling toward her the man she'd feared? His eyes, narrowed and mean, were the only part of him that resembled the intimidating figure she remembered.

"What are you doin' with her? Cosyin' up?" Hector snarled at Jimbo.

"Sharing a pot of coffee," Jimbo replied. "Care to join us?"

"I et breakfast with you the day Miss Prissy arrived in her fancy limo." Hector's hand swiveled around the diner to see who was listening. "Reckon you wanted to gloat, huh, boy? You think cuz she's rich she'll get the farm back for you?" He rocked back on his heels, placed one grimy hand on the table and leaned forward. "You ain't gonna get it, boy. Not even after I heave in my last dyin' breath, unless you start treatin' me like kinfolk should."

Several uncomfortable seconds passed with Jimbo glaring at Hector, Hector giving Caroline a dirty look, and Caroline choking on the memory of Lee using the quitclaim deed on the farm to get even with her for buying Carson Mill.

"Your secret is out," Caroline said, mentally cutting the string on the carrots Hector was about to dangle in front of them. "Lee showed me the quitclaim deed he has on the farm."

Hector muttered a curse that reflected on Lee's parentage. His eyes shifted from his niece to his nephew. "Lee swore me to secrecy. I reckoned he'd be honor bound not to say nothin' either."

Caroline watched her uncle glance nervously over at his shoulder toward the door as though he expected Lee to walk in at any moment. No man called Lee a bastard without paying the price.

"Don't count on anything that isn't in writing," Jimbo said, grinning broadly at his sister. "It takes *two* gentlemen shaking hands to make a gentlemen's agreement. Your deal was one gentleman short."

"Don't you worry none, boy. I got everythin' in writin' all legal-like. The farm is mine till I croak. I even made out a will leavin' my personal belongings to charity. You two ain't gonna get one thin dime cuz you deserted me. Watcha think about that?"

"I think that's why I have a lawyer, Hector. There are loopholes in every legal document, including that quitclaim deed you signed," Caroline replied dryly.

"Yeah, it probably isn't worth the paper it's written on," Jimbo agreed. He reached into his pocket and tossed a twenty-dollar bill on the table. "Go buy yourself a case of rotgut whiskey, old man, and finish drinking yourself to death. We don't need you, the farm or your dimes."

Quicker than a flash of light, Hector snatched the twenty off the table and shoved it into his pocket. "Don't mind if I do, boy. Be seein' you."

"Not if I see him first," Jimbo muttered as Hector ambled away from the table and through the front door. "How did we ever stand sharing a house with that piece of slime?"

"He's ten times worse than he was when we lived at the farm. At least he bathed then." Caroline wrinkled her nose. She could still smell a rancid odor. "I barely recognized him."

"Booze does that to a man," Jimbo said, straightening as he saw Gilda approaching with their breakfast. "It pickled Hector's brain and his body."

"Here you go." Gilda set down the plates as she said, "Eggs over easy for you, Caroline, and a stack of pancakes for you, Jimbo. How's the maple syrup bottle doing? Got plenty?"

"Enough to dull the edge on my sweet tooth," Jimbo answered, holding up the bottle.

"Too bad Lee's off fishin' or something," Gilda commented. "Usually he's real partial to having Sunday breakfast here."

After Gilda left, Jimbo asked, "What's with Gilda and her sudden interest in fishing?"

"Lee and I pulled a prank on her. She overheard a conversation that convinced her there is gold over on the coast."

"Only if you're in the real estate business," Jimbo quipped. "Lee's made a fortune wheeling and dealing in swampland. What do you think the chances are of you being able to coax Lee into parting with that deed?"

Caroline swallowed the bite of egg in her mouth and shook her head. Careful to avoid telling more than she intended, she said, "Lee offered to give it to me."

"You've got it?" Jimbo hooted. "Why didn't you wave it under Hector's nose? He'd have had a conniption fit!"

"Because I didn't accept Lee's—" she paused, searching for a word to substitute for payment for services rendered "—generosity."

Jimbo heard the pause and watched her begin to lavishly butter her biscuit. "I should have known better than to ask. I'm surprised you two stopped squabbling long enough for him to offer the farm to you."

Noticing the smirk on Jimbo's face, Caroline glared at the pat of melting butter. He knew she preferred Gilda's strawberry jam.

"You two always fought like Confederates and Yankees, unless somebody else got either of you in their sights. Then you'd stand back to back and defend each other to the bitter end."

"And you were always neutral," Caroline added, dropping the biscuit on to her plate. She forked a bite of grits into her mouth.

"Neutrality comes with size and age." He cut a wedge of pancakes and shoved it into his mouth. Shifting his food to one side of his mouth, he said, "You have two men protecting your back now."

Do I? The grits suddenly tasted like sawdust rather than ground corn to Caroline. "Last night I broke my dinner engagement with Justin and went with Lee to his house."

"Oh, yeah?"

She stared first at the napkin holder and then at the salt and pepper shakers. She didn't want her eyes to reveal the whole truth to Jimbo. Her brother looked up to her. He'd think less of her if he knew she'd made love to a man who thought she expected payment for services rendered.

"We had what you'd call a major skirmish. On my way back to town, someone tried to run over me on the highway."

Jimbo muffled a curse as he wiped a dribble of maple syrup from the corner of his mouth with his napkin. "Sounds like that tire-slashing. Any idea who it was this time?"

She raised her head until their eyes met. "Lee was furious when I left his place. He wanted to throttle me."

After a short pause, Jimbo shook his head and said quietly, "That isn't exactly a statement of intent to do bodily harm, sis. You're both physical people with quick tempers. If something happened to Lee, you'd probably be at the top of the sheriff's suspect list."

She could avoid telling her brother all that had happened at Lee's house, but the memories of Lee's tender lovemaking caused hope in her voice when she asked, "So you don't think it was Lee?"

"I didn't say that. I've had my ears open, but no one in town seems to know about the vandalism, except for you, me...and Lee. The only gossip I did hear was about you consorting with Justin to buy Whispering Oaks. Which is one more reason for Lee wanting to throttle you." Jimbo studied his sister's face. "Why so bleak? Is there something you haven't told me?"

"I love Lee?" Her subconscious thought broke through the barriers to the conscious level of her mind, startling Caroline. When they'd made love, she'd honestly believed the sizzling sexual chemistry between them was the cause. That, and the guilt feelings she had for neglecting their friendship while she was in Atlanta. It wasn't sex or guilt. She loved him. There was no longer any question in her voice when she repeated the whole truth, "I love him."

"Of course you do," Jimbo agreed, smiling at her. "That goes without saying. You've always loved him."

"No, you don't understand." She sorted through her emotions with the intensity of a seamstress picking at a stubborn knot in a thread. "Before I left, I loved Lee the same way I love you."

"Like a brother?" Jimbo shook his head. "I don't think that's how he felt. I imagine Lee thought of you the same way Carl did."

Caroline's heart sank. "Like my mentor?"

"Like a man feels toward the only woman in his life," Jimbo corrected. "Lee may not have always walked the straight and narrow, but my guess is that he's a one-woman man. You're that woman."

Caroline felt like slapping herself for her own obtuseness. Where was I? she wondered. Why was I blind to how he felt? Had she been standing up too close, or back too far? She hadn't seen the trees for the forest. Lee had offered to marry her twice, but she'd thought he was offering an escape route out of Hector's house. Was it possible that Lee's loving her was the reason he'd given her the quitclaim deed to her mother's land?

"Oh, Jimbo, I've said some awful things to Lee," she whispered in a hushed voice. She put her hands over her face. "Last night, I thought Lee still believed I was a gold digger when he gave me Hector's quitclaim deed. I threw it back in his face."

"Like I said, Lee has plenty of good reasons for wanting to throttle you." He reached across the table, gently tugging Caroline's fingers from her face. "Admit your mistake to him, not me."

"That's easier said than done. What do I say? Hey, Lee, I was at Gilda's having a little chat with Jimbo and realized that I love you. Just to prove it, I'll take the gift I tossed back in your face last night." Caroline groaned softly. "I'd be digging my grave with my own teeth!"

Her self-defeating sarcasm earned her a hard glare from her brother.

"A simple 'I love you' would be better."

"After I practically accused him of running me off the road when he came by the motel?"

Jimbo dropped her hands as he groaned, "You forgot to tell me that minor little detail."

"I guess the only thing I can do is give him time to cool off." And pray his desire for revenge is less than his desire for me, she silently added.

She heard the church bells begin to ring as Jimbo glanced at his wristwatch, then raised his hand to get the check from Gilda.

"After church, why don't we go to the mill?" she suggested. "I'd like your recommendations on the office arrangements."

"Sorry, sis, but I have a long-standing Sunday dinner invitation with a special friend."

"As in female friend?" Her eyes danced wickedly at her brother.

"Uh-huh."

Caroline waited for him to volunteer explicit information. When he didn't, she said, "I bared my soul to you about Lee."

"I hate to quote Gilda, but don't pry. Folks will tell you what they want you to know when they're good and ready." He stopped protesting when he saw Justin enter the door, look around the café, then make a beeline for the booth. "Justin is heading toward us."

"Morning, Caroline," Justin greeted, completely ignoring Jimbo. "You're looking pretty as a wisteria blossom this morning."

"Thanks," Jimbo said with a straight face, but nudging his sister's foot. "You're looking pretty snappy yourself."

Caroline pretended to blot her lips to stifle her laughter. Why hadn't she seen what a pompous ass Justin was years ago? He was standing there, looking down his nose at the Jackson kids the way he'd always done. Only, way back when, she'd mistaken his snooty behavior for sophistication.

"Pardon me for not laughing at your misplaced sense of humor," Justin said, straightening the knot of his tie, then adjusting the cuffs of his white shirt until they were exactly one-half inch below the hem of his jacket sleeve.

"You're pardoned," Jimbo said, dismissing Justin. "Nice talking to you."

"I thought I'd be sociable and offer to take you to church, Caroline," Justin invited. "Afterward, we could go out to Whispering Oaks."

"I thought you took your house off the market last night." Caroline observed Justin's reaction closely. He flinched when she said, "Lee is interested in the old home place."

"So are you," Justin replied candidly.

"Yes, I am. I'd be pleased to go with you when the church service is over. I'll meet you in the motel lobby at noon."

"I'll be there." Justin gave Jimbo a cocky smile, turned and strode triumphantly toward the door.

"You aren't going with him," Jimbo stated bluntly.

Caroline grinned. "I've thought of a way to make up for neglecting Lee all those years, and for buying the mill out from under him. Whispering Oaks is the house he's always wanted, but could never have. I'm the one person who could give the Carson family home to its rightful owner."

"Justin could be the one who ran you off the road last night. Your rejecting his invitation to go with Lee would be enough to make Justin want to scare you out of town."

"He wouldn't kill the goose that's about to lay the golden egg," Caroline argued.

"That's true," Jimbo conceded. "But what if Lee finds out?"

"He won't, unless you tell him."

"Right." Jimbo took a couple of five-dollar bills from his pocket and laid them on the table. "I've got it. See you later, sis." He gave her a quick hug, then shook his finger in front of her face. "In the meantime, you be extra careful."

"I will be," she promised. "I didn't get much sleep last night. After I get back from Whispering Oaks, I'm going straight to bed." She gave her brother a cheeky grin. "I can't get into trouble alone in my own bed, can I?"

Jimbo returned her smile. "If it's possible, you're the one who could do it."

Hours later, Caroline flipped back the bed covers and gave a moan of pleasure as she eased between the sheets. Her eyes, scratchy from lack of sleep and the strain of reading the fine print in Justin's sale contract, instantly closed.

The tour of Whispering Oaks had taken longer than she'd expected. Her lips curved as she visualized the crystal chandelier in the entry hall, sparkling clean, brightly lit. Her imagination led her up the curved oak staircase. A man walked beside her. Tall, erect, with dark hair and gray eyes that shone with love when they looked at her.

"Lee," she whispered sleepily.

Within minutes, exhaustion claimed her. She did not hear the furtive footsteps outside her door, or the motel's master key inserted in her door. Nor did she smell the rancid odor of dirty clothes or the stench of beer. And she didn't feel the sides and foot of the bed being barely lifted until the sheet stretched tautly across all but the arm she'd curved behind her head, or the slightest stirring of air when the pillow beside her head was stealthily lifted from the bed. Not until its softness crushed against her face!

Shocked awake, Caroline tried to jolt upward. She flailed wildly with her left arm, but her right arm and both feet were trapped. She twisted her head from side to side, gulping frantically for air.

"No!" she screamed. Her voice, hoarse with fear, was muffled by the thick foam rubber of the pillow. Precious, life-sustaining air was expelled from her lungs. She'd wasted her breath.

Dammit, she cursed silently as she continued to struggle, she wasn't going to allow herself to be suffocated!

With her free hand, she pushed violently at the arms holding the pillow over her face. A strong callused hand grabbed her wrist, yanking it over her head. Her knuckles cracked against the oak headboard. Pain ricocheted from her fingers down to her shoulder.

But she caught a gasp of air as his weight shifted.

Black spots swam dizzily on the backs of her eyelids. She seemed to see flashes of her life, like black-and-white photographs. Lee carrying her home after she'd skinned her knee playing tag. Lee boosting her up in the oak tree beside the tidal creek. Lee begging her to marry him.

And her refusing him.

Lee! she shrieked silently. Lee!

She broke her wrist free, bent her arm and slammed her elbow against her attacker. Lee would have been proud of her for putting it to good use. She heard the man grunt, felt the pillow shift as his knee buckled against the bed. Her head twisted frantically.

Higher, she thought, her struggles weakening as her lungs seemed to catch fire.

Powered by her will to live, she used her last ounce of strength to lift her shoulder and savagely thrust her elbow at the man. He groaned loudly, momentarily bending forward on her arm. Her fingers clawed the air until she grabbed his cotton shirt. He jerked away.

The pressure was off the pillow. She heard him staggering backward. While she endeavored to push aside the pillow and heave huge wafts of air into her starved lungs, she heard the shuffling of shoe soles on the carpet. The door opened and slammed as a spasm of deep coughs assailed her.

Caroline fought for breath, and gradually the coughing seizure ended. She rolled off the side of the bed, landing on her knees. She felt something hard, twisted, metallic digging into her skin, and reached down to pick it up.

Still warm with body heat, a gold necklace dangled between her fingers, wrapping around her arm like a poisonous snake. She didn't need to turn on the light to recognize it. This wasn't the first time she'd seen it. She'd wound it around her fingertip as she whispered words of love to its owner.

A well of tears spurted from her eyes, coursing unchecked down her cheeks. It was his name she'd called both in ecstasy and in terror. She had dismissed the evidence on three previous occasions. He'd been there when her car was scratched, when her tires were slit, and when the truck had followed her from his house.

A part of her still screamed, "No, it cannot be him!"

Her shoulders drooped. Crumpled in abject defeat, she knew she'd rather have Lee finish his vile deed than know for certain the man she loved had tried to kill her.

Ten

Self-preservation, the strongest instinct, raised Caroline to her knees when she heard a vehicle drive through the parking lot. She inhaled sharply.

Would he dare to come back?

Why not? By now he would have noticed that she'd ripped the gold necklace from his neck. What would he lose by coming back and finishing his dirty work? She could only identify him if she lived through the night!

Fear propelled her upright. She dashed to the door and slid the chain lock in place faster than a machine could wind a bobbin. Hands clasped, knuckles squeezing together, she backed away.

Only then did she notice the necklace wrapped around her fingers. She shook her hands and dropped it as though the herringbone edges were barbed. The gold caught the meager light; it seemed to wink at her. This wasn't a prank she could laugh off!

Her eyes swung back to the only thing between her and disaster. That flimsy chain on the door wouldn't stop him. His muscular shoulders had the power to separate the links easily. Crossing to the drapes, she peeked through a narrow slit. The vehicle hadn't stopped. She could see red taillights far down the road.

Get out of here! Hide!

Where?

While she hurried to the dresser, she whipped her nightgown over her head, flung it aside, then pulled out a pair of jeans and a sweatshirt. Her hands trembled, making it nearly impossible for her to grab the small zipper tab. She failed to close the snap. Her arms and head popped through the shirt's openings as she grabbed her purse.

Heart beating irregularly, she unclasped the chain, turned the knob and made a wild dash for her moped. With trembling hands, she jammed one key into the ignition and tugged on the light switch. ''Get the hell out of town!''

As her headlight beamed through the door she'd left open, the small gold heap on the carpet glimmered. She shook her head.

She wouldn't go back in there for love or money!

A tiny bubble of hysteria parted her lips. Love or money! Either or. The two didn't mix, not for her!

She revved the engine. The tires screeched in protest, as did her heart. Glancing back to see if he was returning, she saw the lights of a truck coming up the street to the back entrance of the parking lot. Quickly, she darted out the front entrance.

The traffic light at the corner of Main Street turned red as she approached. Praying that the sheriff's car would be parked in front of the doughnut shop, she sped through the light. She listened for a siren, watched for the circling blue light, then clenched her hand on the handlebar.

"Graceville is a speeding trap! Where are the cops when I need them?"

Constantly checking behind her, she finally decided she wasn't being followed. She'd gone several miles down the highway before she realized tears were cascading down her cheeks, dripping unnoticed on the front of her sweatshirt. Her hand shook uncontrollably as she wiped them away.

She wasn't going to allow herself to cry!

"I won't shed one damned tear for him!"

Who? You haven't spoken your assailant's name. Why?

She shook her head. She wouldn't listen to her aching heart. "Lee! Lee Carson! Liar extraordinaire! Deceiver of women! Seducer of friends! That's who!"

No.

"Yes!"

No. Trust your heart to know the truth.

"Shut up! I know his necklace when I see it." She bit her lip. Lee Carson wasn't the only man in town who could afford a gold herringbone necklace. "The evidence is stacked against him."

No.

She wiped her hand across her left cheek, then her right cheek. She blinked to clear her vision, but the tears gushed faster. She couldn't think rationally, cry and drive. Now she had eluded her pursuer, driving the moped was at the bottom of her priority list, so she gave a final check behind her, then turned off the highway onto the first narrow lane she saw. If she was going to bawl her eyes out, she had to find a secluded place. She didn't want anyone to see her.

She'd driven less than a quarter of a mile when the familiar broken-down barbed wire fence and the wild growth of briars and brambles began to seem familiar to her. She had no need to look in the distance to know what was ahead of her. Some primitive instinct must have brought her back to the house where she'd been born and raised. She pulled to the side of the lane and cut her lights.

The old place appeared empty and forlorn. Deserted.

A sob broke from deep in her chest. Hot, salty tears she'd suppressed since childhood steadily flowed from her eyes. Dismounting from the moped, she sank to the ground. Her forehead pressed to her knees, her shoulders shaking from the gut-wrenching force of her tears, she cried. Not in fear or bitterness, but in deeply rooted anguish.

She cried over the accident that had taken her father's life when he was her age. She cried for her mother's tragic loss and the hardships she'd endured once Uncle Hector had arrived. She cried for Jimbo's leg being broken.

And she cried for the rash of daily woes she'd had to face that had caused her to be a wild child and troubled teenager. For long, long minutes she indulged in the solace of wallowing in self-pity.

When there were no more tears to cry and her eyes and throat felt scratchy, she slowly started to come to her senses. She wiped her tearstained face on the baggy part of her shirt. Once she'd scrubbed her cheeks, she began to feel marginally better.

After a tremendous sigh, she stood up. She couldn't spend the night camped outside the place where Hector lived. Deciding she'd go to Jimbo's house, she mounted the moped, started the engine and flicked on the headlight.

Every muscle along her spine contracted as she saw Hector Jackson standing on the porch.

Dressed in oversize stained overalls and an undershirt, with a red sweat rag tied haphazardly at his neck, he gestured for her to join him on the porch.

"Come on in and sit for a spell," he called.

He's so scrawny and stoop-shouldered, she thought, just as she had at Gilda's. Was this the man she'd physically feared? The cause of the nightmares that had awakened her many a night in a cold sweat? Why, he's just an old derelict!

Caroline felt like a child shivering in the dark, peeking out from under the covers pulled over her head and staring apprehensively into a dark closet when the light came on. The bogeyman wasn't there. There was nothing to be afraid of.

Feeling less fearful and a little foolish, she turned off the engine and the light. With only the full moon overhead to guide her, she gingerly picked her way through the empty booze bottles Hector must have thrown off the porch when he'd finished drinking the contents.

"'Bout time you paid yer respects," Hector grumbled, opening the screen door and retreating into the house.

Caroline reached out and grabbed the door before it slammed in her face. His manners hadn't improved, she thought, following him inside the house.

The living room had changed. Without her mother or herself to clean and pick up, months—no, years—of junk littered the chairs and tabletops. The only light came from a lamp Jimbo had made; its dusty shade was tilted at an odd angle. The stagnant odor of filth and grime made Caroline want to cover her nose.

"Wanna nip of the hair of the dog?" Hector asked as he splashed three fingers of whiskey into a dirty jelly glass.

"No, thanks."

"Always was prissy," Hector mumbled, his words slurring together. He drained the glass in two gulps. "Uptight. Like that bastard who stole the farm from me."

Caroline felt the hairs on the back of her neck rise. Hector was drunk! What was she doing here? Of all people, she knew from experience Hector turned mean when he'd had too much to drink.

"I'd better go. It's late."

Too late, she thought when his hand reached out, quicker than a snake striking, and pushed her. The back of her knees hit the sofa cushion. She fell backward, hard, bouncing to one side.

"Sit," Hector ordered. "You ain't goin' anywhere until we've had us a friendly little reunion."

In the blink of an eye, she saw herself as a child cornered on this same sofa, with Hector bellowing at her.

"You ain't got no secrets from me, girlie. I know 'bout you and him. I seen you makin' eyes at him right out in the middle of the square in front of God 'n everybody." Hector snickered. "That's why I scritched yer car 'n slit yer tires." He shook his tobacco-stained finger at her. "I know what you was up to at his house—'suadin' him to sign my farm over to you."

"It was you!" Caroline whispered her accusation. Was he the one who had forced her off the road? Who had tried to murder her tonight? Her mouth felt as though she'd eaten a bale of cotton. She glanced from Hector to the screen door, wondering if she could get out of there before he could catch her. Hector was a braggart. She had to keep him talking. "You've been following me?"

"Scairt you, didn't I?"

When he grinned, Caroline noticed he'd lost a front tooth. The smell of his rancid breath made her gag.

"Yer scairt now!" he gloated.

"No," she denied with false bravado. "You don't scare me."

"Sure do," Hector argued. His speech slurred further. "Don't you lie to yer ol' Uncle Hector. You think yer smart. Smart as them 'spensive lawyers you bragged 'bout. But I'm smarter 'n you, Miss Fancy-pants."

Caroline watched his eyes narrow. It's now or never, she thought, pushing off the sofa to make a dash for the door.

She screamed when Hector grabbed her wrist and shoved her backward. His fingers bit into her flesh. She'd misjudged his strength and agility.

"Let go of me, Hector!"

She heard the pound of feet on the porch. The door swung open so hard it nearly fell off its rusty hinges. Hector pulled her against him, wrapping his arm around her neck.

"Let her go," Lee ordered.

Caroline squirmed to be free; Hector tightened his arm. Her eyes fell from Lee's stormy gray eyes to his bare neck.

No necklace.

Her uncle had admitted to the acts of vandalism, but not to attempted murder.

"I didn't do nothin' to her," Hector whined. "Jest scairt her a little. Didn't mean her no harm. You back on outta here 'n I'll let her go in a minute or two."

Lee held out his hand toward her. "She comes with me."

The arm around Caroline's neck loosened. It was her choice. She could stay or leave.

Lee Carson had been her nemesis. But he had also been her champion, and recently her lover, her only lover. Instinctively, she knew whom to trust.

She broke free of Hector's hold and took Lee's hand.

"Stay away from my woman, Hector," Lee warned as he put his arm protectively around Caroline's shoulders. "If I so much as suspect you're within a ten-mile radius of her, you won't have to worry about who lives and dies on her farm. I personally guarantee that you won't be buried on it. Do you hear me loud and clear?"

Hector visibly shrank. His shoulders slouched; his head lolled from side to side. "Uh-huh. I heard you," he mewled.

Caroline hugged Lee's waist. "Get me out of here. Take me home where I belong, Lee, please."

Within scant minutes, they were in Lee's truck and driving down the lane.

Lee had one eye on the bumpy road and one eye on Caroline. He wanted to hold her, to reassure her that she was safe, but this wasn't the time or the place. She'd begged him to take her home, and he knew there was only one place she'd call home...Atlanta.

She was huddled against the door because his love hadn't been strong enough to protect her. He couldn't blame her for wanting to leave.

To no avail he'd tried to stop her once. He'd learned from his mistakes. What was her favorite motto? She decided who and where and when. Well, he wasn't the who. Graceville wasn't the where. And now wasn't the when. It ripped at the seams of his heart to even think about her leaving him, but all the love he felt for her couldn't force her to stay.

"I'm sorry, Caroline. This could have been avoided. It's my fault."

"Your fault?"

"Yeah. I let my feelings for Justin blind me to what was going on. After I gave Hector the cash to pay off the notes, I had a string of 'accidents' happen to me. I warned Hector, and they stopped." Lee halted the truck as he reached the blacktop road. To the left was Graceville and his house, to the right was Atlanta. One last desperate hope prevented him from turning toward Atlanta. He'd jumped to the wrong conclusions about her before. This time, he had to hear it coming from her own lips. "Where to, Caroline?"

There was only one place Caroline would feel completely safe—in Lee's arms, at his home. "Home, where I belong," she said softly, praying that all that had passed between them had not made this impossible.

Lee felt as if he had just died. Caroline wanted to leave him again, and this time was far worse than the first. "You're sure?" was all he said, however.

"Positive," Caroline said. She hoped to see a flash of the whiteness of his teeth, but instead he turned his face to check for oncoming traffic. When he checked in her direction, he smiled, but the smile didn't reach his eyes. She waited for him to pull out onto the road, but he didn't put the truck in gear.

He must know I thought it was him for a few irrational minutes, she concluded suddenly. But that wasn't fair. When the cards were down, she *had* trusted him. She'd literally put her life in his hands when all the evidence was stacked against him. Surely he would realize that.

"I found your necklace on the floor after Hector tried to smother me with the pillow," she said.

Lee nodded. Unable to push sounds past the lump clogging his throat, he put his hand in his shirt pocket and held the necklace out to her. He swallowed hard. "I found it in your room. When I saw the door left open, I knew you must be in danger."

Puzzled, Caroline asked, "But how did you know where I was?"

"I'd been getting prank phone calls. When I answered, the line would be dead. The same thing happened back when I'd had problems with Hector before, but it wasn't until I was getting ready for bed and noticed that my necklace was missing off the nightstand that I put two and two together. I don't always put the security system on, and Hector had sneaked in once before. When I saw the necklace gone, I figured he was up to no good and trying to implicate me. Then you weren't in the motel and the door was open, so I feared the worst, and went right out to the farm."

He held out the necklace to Caroline. "I bought this necklace the same day I got the quitclaim deed on the farm. You always admired the ribbons the girls used to wear to school. I thought you'd like the idea of a long ribbon of gold around your neck."

Caroline caught the necklace as he dropped it into her hand. He hadn't gotten the sequence of events quite right, but she didn't care. The gold of the necklace conducted the heat from his hand straight to her heart.

"A satin ribbon would have been fine, Lee." She let the length of gold dangle from her hand, then put it over his head.

"Satin isn't good enough for you. I would have bought pearls or diamonds or emeralds, but I couldn't afford them back then."

Her fingers traced the chain as it lay on his neck. "Despite what you think, money doesn't buy my love. I know you still believe I married Carl for his money."

"Shh, Caroline." He put his arm around her shoulders to draw her close to him. "You're upset. You don't have to tell me any of this."

"I want you to understand why he married me, why I married him. It doesn't matter to me what others think, but I can't let you go on believing I married Carl for his money."

She felt Lee's fingers slide from her arm to her waist, pulling her tightly against him. She paused, inhaling a shaky breath before she explained her reasons for marrying Carl. "I loved him."

"Caroline, stop." The first three words of her reason for marrying Carl Noble were more than he wanted to hear. She could call it selfishness, denial or plain old stubborn craziness, but he'd heard three words too many! "You've had the hell scared out of you by Hector. That's enough stress for one night."

Caroline grabbed his arm. "So help me Hannah, Lee Carson, you're going to listen to me tell you about Carl Noble if I have to hog-tie you and shout the truth in your ears."

"I told you I don't want to hear it. Carl was an old man who wanted a young bride. You both got what you wanted. You're here and you're safe. Forget everything else!"

She couldn't forget it. She needed him to understand. "Carl did not marry me because he wanted me to share his bed!"

"I can't imagine any man not wanting you," Lee said, completely baffled.

She tugged on his arm until Lee glanced over at her. "Carl was my friend, my mentor."

"So was I. That wasn't a good enough reason for you to marry me."

"No, it wasn't. The first time you proposed, it was because Hector made me drop out of school. Remember?"

"Yes, but—"

"The second time you proposed was after Justin's surprise birthday party. You proposed to keep me from running off to Atlanta."

"I loved you, dammit!"

Caroline smiled sadly. "I didn't know that."

"Would it have made a difference if I'd told you?"

She didn't want to hurt his feelings, but she had to be honest with him. "Probably not. I was headstrong, hell-bent on shaking the red dust of Graceville off my shoes. Nobody and nothing was going to keep me here. So I ran away.''

"And never looked back," Lee said bitterly, remembering how hurt he'd been when he had to pump Jimbo for information about her. "Except for keeping contact with Jimbo, you might as well have stepped off the edge of the world."

Detecting the hurt in his voice, she laced her fingers in his. "I was struggling to survive. I had to block home and everybody here out of my mind or I'd have given up and returned. I'd have failed, lost what little self-confidence I had in myself. I nearly reached that point many times before Carl took me under his wing." She squeezed Lee's hand, hoping he understood she'd never meant to cause him pain. "Carl knew he was dying when he convinced me to marry him. I was the daughter he'd never had. He was the father I'd always been denied. He wanted me to have everything we'd worked together to earn."

She gave him a straight look. "I won't lie and say the thought of being financially secure repelled me. Of course it didn't. You show me somebody who has gone to bed hungry, or worn the same threadbare coat until the hem of the sleeve reached her elbow, who says she isn't concerned about security and I'll show you a liar."

"Wealth and security aren't the same. I could have provided you with security."

Caroline dropped his hand to rub the knot of tension forming at the back of her neck. "I refused you because I had to break the cycle of poverty—school dropout, early marriage, babies, then watching those babies grow up, drop out of school, marry young, have babies and on and on and on. I wanted a better life, for me and for my children. I don't regret marrying Carl. He gave me far, far more than money. We had a very special relationship."

Her hand moved over her heart as she raised her eyes, silently hoping Carl wouldn't feel betrayed by what she was about to say. "While my marriage lacked passion and physical intimacy, that doesn't make what we felt for each other a cheap imitation of love. Carl wasn't physically able, but if he had been we would have shared the same bedroom."

Lee's eyes locked on Caroline's face. His mind raced backward. No passion! No physical intimacy! Carl had not made love to her!

Caroline couldn't understand why Lee was staring at her the way he was. She had wanted to explain the way she really felt, but Lee seemed stunned. "Lee?" she asked.

His voice showed his complete disbelief. "Are you telling me you were a virgin? When we made love, I thought for a moment you were. But I knew I must have imagined it."

"Is that possible?"

"It is for a man who had vivid dreams of making love to you when you were hundreds of miles from his bed. That was physically impossible, too."

He smiled for the first time. Reaching over, he folded her into his arms. "The tricks a man's mind will play."

Caroline snuggled against him, feeling safe for the first time since Hector's attack. "Let's go back to your house, Lee."

He stared at her in shock. "My house? You said you wanted to go to Atlanta."

"No. I said I wanted to go home...."

"To my house?" He wasn't taking even the slimmest chance on being wrong.

"Where I belong. Isn't that with you?"

Lee's breath caught in his throat when he saw the tears glistening in her eyes. He could cope with her tears of joy, but not ones caused by sadness. His hand framed her face as he asked, "Is that where you want to be? With me? Now?"

"Yes." To alleviate any doubts he had, she lightly brushed her lips against his mouth. Her hand stroked the long length of his thigh. "Please, take me home."

The fear embedded in his soul demanded to be set free from worry. "You won't run away?"

"Only if you go with me."

A shudder rippled through Lee, leaving him weak as a newborn babe. He laced his fingers through hers and brought them to his parted lips. Her polished nails felt sleek against the rough edges of his teeth as he gently nipped each of her fingers. He whispered his love against her palm, then curled her fingers around it for safekeeping.

"Let's go home," he murmured.

To Caroline, the short drive seemed a million miles long. The landscape lights lining the path to the front door seemed the right distance for a landing strip at Atlanta's airport. The short flight of steps leading to the master bedroom seemed steeper than those leading to heaven.

Time had ceased to exist in the closed room. Lee's robe lay across the foot of the bed where she'd left it. Without lifting the pillow, she knew the deed to the farm remained where she'd angrily shoved it. Her gaze fell to the strand of red satin ribbon that had fallen from her lap to the carpet.

Sensitive to her slightest movement or glance, Lee strode to the place where her eyes focused and picked up the ribbon. His hand trembled as he held it out to her. When she moved beside him with her palm turned upward, he let the thread of satin gently loop across the lifeline on her palm, the place he'd kissed.

"I didn't lie to you about my reasons for getting the deed to the Jackson farm. I left it on your pillow because I believed it showed how much I love you."

Caroline smiled up at him. "You'll remember those reasons tomorrow morning when you wake up and find the bill of sale for Whispering Oaks on your pillow, won't you?"

For an instant she thought she'd chosen the wrong time to tell him. He grabbed her arms and pulled her to him.

"A gift of love?" he asked, his voice thick with emotion.

"Yes." Impatiently, she began unbuttoning his shirt. She thrust her hands inside his shirt, loving the texture of his hot bare skin. "Fix it up...tear it down...whatever you want. It's yours. Justin is leaving Graceville."

He whispered her name as he covered her mouth with a searing kiss and fell to the bed.

How could he thank her? She'd given him more than bricks and mortar. She'd given him his roots. As she sensuously moved against him, he tangled his fingers into the silky softness of her hair, parting their mouths so he could look into her blue eyes.

The love he saw there restored his childhood belief that anything was possible with her beside him.

"Between the two of us, Caroline, we can build a whole new town, a better town. It'll be different. We won't be stuck on the outside looking in . . . we won't be misfits any longer."

Caroline shifted to her side, then contoured her body against Lee, leaving only enough room for her hand to roam freely over his chest, waist and hip. She tugged at his belt buckle and released the snap of his slacks. It took a conscious effort for her to part the zipper slowly, one tooth at a time.

"Neither of us is a misfit when we're together," she said, as she kicked off her sandals and trekked her bare toes up the outside seam of his slacks.

His lips hovered over hers, touched, then hovered again, delaying, tantalizing. He teased her mouth with his tongue and teeth, letting their breaths mingle until their thoughts focused entirely on giving each other pleasure.

A whisper of encouragement, a shudder, the shifting of arms and legs—these were only small parts of their secret language of love that allowed them to shed their clothing with style and grace.

"Here?" Caroline asked, circling the puckered edge of his flat nipple with her finger. His chest muscles tensed as she evoked the same exquisite sensation he caused by touching her breasts. She heard him take a sharp breath as the pointed tip of her tongue replaced the oval edge of her fingernail. "Yes?"

Lee swept his hand along the hollow of her back, squeezing her bottom, then lightly touching her behind her knees. He felt her smile as she peppered kisses across his chest. "Ticklish?"

"You know I am."

Yes, he knew of other spots, but not there. "Let me kiss them."

"The back of my knees?"

"Mmm."

She rolled to her stomach, trusting Lee, willing to try anything within reason. She felt his chin lightly sandpaper the crease, then his lips gently caressed the abrasion. What she'd thought would cause laughter made her toes curl and her buttocks clench.

A low groan escaped from between her lips as he repeated the movements along her calves. When he bent her leg and kissed the arch of her foot, she began wadding the sheet in her hands as a series of delicious tremors ran up her legs.

"Enough," she whispered weakly. After she'd turned over to her back, she asked, "Did you know what that would do to me?"

Lee shook his head. His voice was rough with passion when he said, "Or to me."

She drew him down on top of her, wrapping her legs around him, holding him securely against her, wanting him to assuage the ache he'd caused by his unorthodox lovemaking. Her eyes floated closed as he rocked against her, parting the delicate folds of flesh, but steadfastly refusing to become part of her.

"Lee," she cried, feeling a seizure of tiny convulsions building in her. She twisted against him. "Don't make me wait. You're driving me crazy!"

If this was craziness, Lee willingly crossed over the brink into the sweet heat of delirious insanity. Shaking with a mindless rapture, he thrust into her.

Her incredible softness combined with her searing heat made the pleasure so intense, he gasped, "It's— never been—like this. I can't—hold—back."

He braced his arms, locking the muscles in his chest, abdomen and thighs to gain control. He would have withdrawn, but Caroline's legs were wrapped tightly around him and snared him in his own weakness. When she arched against him and he felt her climax, he erupted with savage intensity.

Caroline cuddled next to Lee. Sketching lazy paisley-print shapes at the edge of the gold chain around his neck, she asked, "Is it different every time?"

"Yes," he replied succinctly. Silently, he was posing a question to himself. Should he risk a fatal blow to his self-esteem by proposing marriage...again? His answer was the same as to Caroline's question. He threaded his hands through her hair with the same careful deliberation a farsighted person used while threading the small eye of a quilting needle. "Will you marry me, Caroline Jackson Noble?"

Her heart brimmed with joy, spilling over in the form of tears. She gave him the answer he'd wanted to hear the day she'd boarded the bus for Atlanta. "Yes, Lee. I want to marry you."

Lee bent and kissed away the tear clinging to her eyelashes. His lips gently brushed against her cheek and temple. "I love you, Caroline. Hold on to me, sweetheart, and let me hold on to you. I'll never let you go again."

Caroline's arms closed around the man she loved. She felt safe and secure...and loved. At last, she'd come home.

*   *   *   *   *

The spirit of motherhood is the spirit of love—and how better to capture that special feeling than in our short story collection...

Curtiss Ann Matlock
Carole Halston
Linda Shaw

Three glorious new stories that embody the very essence of family and romance are contained in this heartfelt tribute to Mother. Share in the joy by joining us and three of your favorite Silhouette authors for this celebration of motherhood and romance.

Available at your favorite retail outlet in May.

SMD92

NORA ROBERTS

Love has a language all its own, and for centuries, flowers have symbolized love's finest expression. Discover the language of flowers—and love—in this romantic collection of 48 favorite books by bestselling author Nora Roberts.

Two titles are available each month at your favorite retail outlet.

In April, look for:

First Impressions, **Volume #5**
Reflections, **Volume #6**

In May, look for:

Night Moves, **Volume #7**
Dance of Dreams, **Volume #8**

Collect all 48 titles and become fluent in

THE LANGUAGE of LOVE

LOL 492

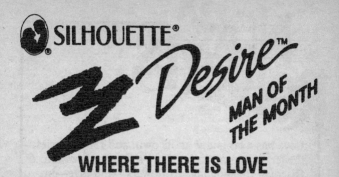

WHERE THERE IS LOVE

Annette Broadrick

Secret agent Max Moran knew all too well the rules of a road where life-threatening danger lurked around every corner. He stalked his prey like a panther—silent, stealthy and ready to spring at any moment.

But teaming up again with delicate, determined Marisa Stevens meant tackling a far more tortuous terrain—one that Max had spent a lifetime avoiding. This precariously unpredictable path was enough to break the stoic panther's stride... as it wove its way to where there was love.

Last sighted in CANDLELIGHT FOR TWO (Silhouette Desire #577), the mysterious Max is back as Silhouette's *Man of the Month!* Don't miss Max's story, WHERE THERE IS LOVE by Annette Broadrick, available in May... only from Silhouette Desire.

SDAB

"GET AWAY FROM IT ALL" SWEEPSTAKES

HERE'S HOW THE SWEEPSTAKES WORKS

NO PURCHASE NECESSARY

To enter each drawing, complete the appropriate Official Entry Form or a 3" by 5" index card by hand-printing your name, address and phone number and the trip destination that the entry is being submitted for (i.e., Caneel Bay, Canyon Ranch or London and the English Countryside) and mailing it to: Get Away From It All Sweepstakes, P.O. Box 1397, Buffalo, New York 14269-1397.

No responsibility is assumed for lost, late or misdirected mail. Entries must be sent separately with first class postage affixed, and be received by: 4/15/92 for the Caneel Bay Vacation Drawing, 5/15/92 for the Canyon Ranch Vacation Drawing and 6/15/92 for the London and the English Countryside Vacation Drawing. Sweepstakes is open to residents of the U.S. (except Puerto Rico) and Canada, 21 years of age or older as of 5/31/92.

For complete rules send a self-addressed, stamped (WA residents need not affix return postage) envelope to: Get Away From It All Sweepstakes, P.O. Box 4892, Blair, NE 68009.

© 1992 HARLEQUIN ENTERPRISES LTD.   SWP-RLS

"GET AWAY FROM IT ALL" SWEEPSTAKES

HERE'S HOW THE SWEEPSTAKES WORKS

NO PURCHASE NECESSARY

To enter each drawing, complete the appropriate Official Entry Form or a 3" by 5" index card by hand-printing your name, address and phone number and the trip destination that the entry is being submitted for (i.e., Caneel Bay, Canyon Ranch or London and the English Countryside) and mailing it to: Get Away From It All Sweepstakes, P.O. Box 1397, Buffalo, New York 14269-1397.

No responsibility is assumed for lost, late or misdirected mail. Entries must be sent separately with first class postage affixed, and be received by: 4/15/92 for the Caneel Bay Vacation Drawing, 5/15/92 for the Canyon Ranch Vacation Drawing and 6/15/92 for the London and the English Countryside Vacation Drawing. Sweepstakes is open to residents of the U.S. (except Puerto Rico) and Canada, 21 years of age or older as of 5/31/92.

For complete rules send a self-addressed, stamped (WA residents need not affix return postage) envelope to: Get Away From It All Sweepstakes, P.O. Box 4892, Blair, NE 68009.

© 1992 HARLEQUIN ENTERPRISES LTD.   SWP-RLS

"GET AWAY FROM IT ALL"

Brand-new Subscribers-Only Sweepstakes
OFFICIAL ENTRY FORM

This entry must be received by: April 15, 1992
This month's winner will be notified by: April 30, 1992
Trip must be taken between: May 31, 1992—May 31, 1993

YES, I want to win the Caneel Bay Plantation vacation for two. I understand the prize includes round-trip airfare and the two additional prizes revealed in the BONUS PRIZES insert.

Name _____

Address _____

City _____

State/Prov._____ Zip/Postal Code_____

Daytime phone number _____
                              (Area Code)

Return entries with invoice in envelope provided. Each book in this shipment has two entry coupons — and the more coupons you enter, the better your chances of winning!
© 1992 HARLEQUIN ENTERPRISES LTD.   1M-CPN